D1006981

TAKING A CHANCE ON LOVE

OTHER BOOKS BY
MARY RAZZELL

Snow Apples, Groundwood, 1984; 2006

The Secret Code of DNA, Penumbra, 1986

Salmonberry Wine, Groundwood, 1987

Night Fires, Groundwood, 1990

White Wave, Groundwood, 1994

Smuggler's Moon, Groundwood, 1999

Haida Quest, Harbour Publishing, 2002

Runaway at Sea, Harbour Publishing, 2005

Dreaming of Horses, Dragon Hill Publishing, 2013

Taking a Chance on Love

Mary Razzell

RONSDALE PRESS

TAKING A CHANCE ON LOVE
Copyright © 2016 Mary Razzell

RONSDALE PRESS
3350 West 21st Avenue, Vancouver, B.C., Canada V6S 1G7
www.ronsdalepress.com

Typesetting: Julie Cochrane, in Minion 12 pt on 16
Cover Art & Design: Elisa Gutiérrez
Paper: Ancient Forest Friendly "Silva" (FSC)—100% post-consumer waste,
    totally chlorine-free and acid-free

Ronsdale Press wishes to thank the following for their support of its publishing
program: the Canada Council for the Arts, the Government of Canada through the
Canada Book Fund, the British Columbia Arts Council, and the Province of British
Columbia through the British Columbia Book Publishing Tax Credit program.

Library and Archives Canada Cataloguing in Publication

Razzell, Mary, 1930–, author
    Taking a chance on love / Mary Razzell. — First edition.

Issued in print and electronic formats.
ISBN 978-1-55380-455-0 (paperback)
ISBN 978-1-55380-456-7 (ebook) / ISBN 978-1-55380-457-4 (pdf)

    I. Title.

PS8585.A99T35 2016   jC813'.54   C2015-906728-6   C2015-906729-4

At Ronsdale Press we are committed to protecting the environment. To this end we
are working with Canopy and printers to phase out our use of paper produced from
ancient forests. This book is one step towards that goal.

Printed in Canada by Marquis Printing, Quebec

for Nina Ruman,
the best of friends

ACKNOWLEDGEMENTS

With special thanks to Helen Shore, BScN, for her recollections of the burn ward at the Vancouver General Hospital in 1944–45. And to Joe Holmes of Richmond, B.C., collector and restorer of Easthope engines.

This is a work of fiction and any resemblance to anyone living or dead is coincidental.

Chapter One

✻

I WAS THE ONE WHO found the first note. My friend Amy and I had just been dropped off from the school bus and were dawdling along the road to my house when I had to take a short trip into the woods to answer nature's call. The sun shone on the new leaves of alder trees, and on the way back to Amy, I stopped to smell the freshness of the spring air.

There it was, partially tucked under a flat rock, a small piece of white paper torn from a notepad and folded in half. It couldn't have been there long because the paper wasn't wet, and it had stopped raining only half an hour before.

I read it quickly and called to Amy as I came out to the road.

"You'll never guess what I found!"

Amy Miller and I were the only two girls living in the Landing. We went to high school by bus to the next village up the coast. Once school was out, and we were back home, we had only each other to rely on for company. Amy and I were both seventeen and in grade eleven.

Amy knew all about clothes and makeup. She looked like Hedy Lamarr, except she was blonde. She had the same gorgeous figure: a small waist and high, rounded breasts that made all the men in the village stop and follow her with their eyes. The women frowned.

Ever since the summer before, when Amy had moved to the Landing, we had seen each other every day. She was a good listener, and I could talk to her about anything. The very worst thing that I could imagine would be to lose Amy as my friend.

I read aloud the note I'd found. "What happened to you yesterday? I waited as long as I could. R."

"Let me see, Meg," said Amy, her face clouding. "It sounds like a love note."

"Could be." I gave her the note. "Do you recognize the handwriting? I think it looks like a man's. Heavy scrawl and messy, just like my brother, Sam's." Sam was my oldest brother and away in the war. He had joined the Air Force in 1940, soon after Canada had declared war on Germany.

Amy's face crumpled, and she looked ready to cry. She kept smoothing the note over and over with her right index finger, as if she were trying to erase the words. I couldn't understand why she was upset.

"It could be Rob Pryce," she said. "He gave my mother a card on April Fool's day. He wrote on it, 'Just for fun.' The writing looked like this."

"I don't like him," I said. "I hate the way he looks at me, as if he's taking off all my clothes."

Robert Pryce. He and his family had moved to the Landing just after Christmas. We thought they must be rich. No one in their family seemed to work, and they had the nicest house in the village. A creek ran the length of the property, right down to the beach, and their view went all the way out to the Gap, and beyond, to Vancouver Island. Rob had a pretty wife, a little younger. She was from a prominent Toronto family. Some said that Rob was a writer, or an artist, or maybe both. Others said he was a Communist. He was the handsomest man on the peninsula in an Errol Flynn sort of way. He had brothers who visited occasionally, and they were all good-looking. There was a sister, too, but the good looks didn't work as well on her. Everyone on the peninsula took note of the Pryce men.

Robert Pryce reminded me of my own father, who was away in the Air Force on the East Coast. Dad had always had an eye for the women. Mild flirtations going on whenever a chance presented itself. I had long ago decided I didn't like men like that.

"I could check under the rock every time I go by here," I

said now to Amy. "It's close to my house. And I'll keep a look-out for whoever is walking this way."

"I wonder who it could be? But maybe it doesn't mean anything." Amy's face relaxed at the thought.

"Probably not."

"Let's keep the note anyway, Meg. Just to see what happens."

"You keep it," I said. "My mother's always looking through my things, and she'd find this. She would throw a fit."

"No, you keep it."

I looked at her in surprise. "Why?"

But she wouldn't tell me, and I let it go.

As soon as I got home, I put the note in my new hiding place, under a loose floorboard in my bedroom.

Neither of us expected to find a second note the very next day. We'd missed the school bus because of basketball practice and had to walk home, so we were later than usual. Only a corner of white paper showed from under the rock.

"It looks like it's been torn from the same notebook," said Amy.

We read it out loud together. "S, please get in touch."

"Maybe he knows someone took his first note," I said.

"No initial 'R' this time," said Amy. "Is that an 'S' or a '5'?"

"Who would start a note with a '5'? Can you think of a female within walking distance whose first name starts with 'S'?"

Amy shook her head.

Ours was a small fishing village along the B.C. coast, and it didn't take long to think of all the women under the age of fifty whose name started with "S." We came up with three. All of them were married.

"Let's watch them," said Amy. "See where they go out walking. Are they buying new clothes? Wearing more makeup than usual?"

"Sylvia Ballard," we both said.

"Did I tell you that last week Mrs. Ballard was wearing Evening in Paris perfume in the store?" said Amy. "As if she were going on a date afterwards. Maybe it was a date with Robert Pryce."

"How was she dressed?"

"You know that red angora sweater she has, the turtleneck?" Amy said. "Someone should tell her that she's too old to wear that colour. Too bright. Makes her look haggard. She'd be better off with a soft coral. It's more becoming to all ages."

"I think red's okay for evening," I said. "The last time I saw her wear it was when she went out to the movies with her husband, and I was babysitting. I thought she looked okay."

"If we take this note, he probably won't leave any more," Amy said. "Should we leave it?"

"Leave it," I said.

"No, I have an idea," said Amy. "This one I'll keep."

The next morning on the school bus, Amy seemed upset. She was scowling and kept twisting her hair around her finger.

"Guess who was at my house after I left you yesterday?" she said. "Robert Pryce. It seems he's always there. Said he was helping my mother fill out some forms for the government. Why couldn't she wait for my dad to help her? He'll be up this weekend. Anyway, I checked out Robert Pryce's handwriting on the forms, and it's the very same handwriting that's on the notes."

"Have you noticed how he's always super helpful to all the women?" I said. "Anyway, when Robert Pryce sees your dad is home, he might back off. At least, you know that 'S' isn't your mother, not with a name like Norma. Once we find out who 'S' is, maybe we can do something about it and show Robert Pryce up for the creep he is."

After school that day, I came home to find my mother sitting at the kitchen table reading the first note Amy and I had found.

"What's this all about?" she said. "It must be important for you to hide it away. I want to know every detail, don't leave anything out. And by the way, it wouldn't hurt you to mop under your bed."

"Mom!"

"I would never have found it if the cat hadn't been sneezing with all the dust under your bed. Thick as a blanket. The floorboard was loose."

"Amy and I found the note in the woods, and we've been trying to figure out who 'S' is."

"It's nothing for you to involve yourself in, Meg. You or Amy." She glanced at the note again. "But it does make you wonder." Her eyes sharpened. "I have half a notion it has something to do with one of the Pryce men. I've never liked their looks. Half the women in the village are acting dotty because of them. I hope you'll take this as a warning and not let yourself be one of them."

When the *Lady Alexandra* docked at the Landing that Friday night, crowded with the usual weekenders from the city, I spotted Amy's father among them. I'd met him before — he came to the Landing about twice a month — and once again I was struck by how much alike he and Amy looked. They both had thick blonde hair, the same dark, arching eyebrows and eyes blue as the mountains on a September morning. As soon as Mr. Miller stepped off the gangplank, he hugged Amy. Amy's mother wasn't there to meet the boat, but that wasn't surprising. Amy had told me the first time we met that her mother had high blood pressure and didn't go out much.

She'd said, "It's really the reason we moved here. The doctors said she needed to be out of the stress of the city."

Amy's face was bright with happiness as she and her father walked up the wharf together. I knew that she loved her father almost to the point of worship, but seeing her face now, so radiant with love, made me swallow hard. Even though I didn't like the way my father acted around other women, I missed him. Most of the time, I was able to push the feeling down to a dull ache.

Amy didn't seem to see me, she was so taken up with her father. I wondered if I should call on her in the morning as I always did.

Just when I had decided I wouldn't, she turned around and called over her shoulder, "See you tomorrow, Meg."

"Sure," I called back, happy again.

The next day I took the shortcut from the main road up to the secondary road and then up the few steps over the drainage ditch to Amy's cottage. I had been to her house so often, my feet knew every stone. Wild broom on either side of the path quivered with bees, dizzy with the scent of the red-streaked yellow blossoms.

Amy answered the door. The house smelled of bacon and coffee, and Mr. Miller was still eating at the table in the living room. Mrs. Miller was all dressed up in a matching sweater set, a pale blue that made her red hair glow in contrast. Usually, I would find her lying on the living room couch wearing an old ratty sweater with pills of wool that my fingers longed to pick off. She would have a cup of tea beside her and a stack of magazines and books to read as she rested.

"My mother has to lie down as much as possible," Amy had once said. "That's what old Doc Casey told her."

Mrs. Miller had a petite figure and giggled. She treated me as if I were a younger sister that she liked, and I couldn't help liking her back. Amy didn't like her mother, though.

Once I asked her why, and she'd said, "I hate the way she treats my father."

"What do you mean?"

"She should be nicer to him. Not take him for granted."

I said to Amy now, "Let's go down to the beach."

The tide was out when we got there, and the smell of seaweed mingled with the tang of salt water. A tugboat, its diesel engines throbbing, edged past Keats Island on its way to the pulp mill at Port Mellon. Amy and I scrunched down into the sand and leaned against one of the silvered logs. I closed my eyes against the sun.

"You know what I'd like more than anything?" said Amy dreamily.

"What? What would you like more than anything?" said a man's deep voice.

Robert Pryce. He had his dog, a young German shepherd, with him, and they both sat down beside us. That is, Robert Pryce sat next to Amy. I thought of what my mother had said about Amy soon after the Millers had moved to the Landing.

"That young girl attracts too much male attention, in my opinion."

Robert shifted his weight until his leg touched Amy's. I waited for her to pull hers away. She didn't. I remembered my mother warning me once, "Don't let any man get too familiar with you, or touch you. Trouble lies that way." My tongue was dry and stuck to the roof of my mouth when I saw how Amy leaned in closer to Robert.

Robert stayed with us for about fifteen minutes. He and Amy chatted away about nothing at all important, but it seemed charged with an undercurrent of excitement. I felt shut out, a hundred years old, ugly, unwanted: incredible feelings I'd never had before. How two people talking in the sun could make me feel that way, I would never have imagined. When Robert got up to leave, I was glad.

Even though Amy and I spent the rest of the afternoon together, I couldn't shake the disturbed feeling that I had watched my best friend begin a game whose rules I didn't understand.

Chapter Two

❧

I MET SYLVIA BALLARD in the village store that Saturday morning. Smiling, she came over to me. "Are you free to baby-sit tonight at seven-thirty? My husband and I have decided at the last minute we'd like to go to the dance at the Legion in Gibson's." Since Amy and I had put Mrs. Ballard at the top of our list of suspects, I was quick to say yes.

That evening as soon as I had Joanie, the Ballards' five-year-old, in bed — and it seemed to take hours with her wanting endless drinks of water, and "just one more story" — I began to look for clues. There weren't any that I could find.

I looked everywhere but the parents' bedroom. All I discovered was that Sylvia Ballard liked *True Confessions* magazines and hid them in the deep kitchen drawer that also held a twenty-pound bag of white Five Roses flour. I learned, too, that Mr. Ballard liked to leave little love notes lying around for his wife and that he called her "Bunnykins." It didn't seem to fit with his bald head and long, gangly frame.

Amy and I talked about it after school on Monday.

"There was just the usual junk lying around the desk and kitchen counters," I said. "Bills and stuff like that."

"Did you check her jacket pockets? She always wears that red plaid one when she goes for a walk." Amy loved clothes.

"I didn't think of it," I said. "Joanie was being a real brat. I was looking for something to eat, and she called out, 'I heard you open the fridge door, and I'm going to tell my mother.' She's spoiled rotten. My mother says it's because she's an only child."

Amy looked at me, annoyance flickering in her eyes. Too late, I remembered that Amy was an only child. "I like being an only child," she'd once said.

"Your dad get away to the city all right?" I asked.

"Yes. And the *Lady Alexandra* had barely pulled out when you-know-who came to visit. I answered the door, and you'll never guess what he said to me. He said, 'You're even prettier than your mother.'" Amy looked pleased. "Of course, my dad thinks so, too."

I looked at her in surprise. "That's stupid," I said. "She's your mother, not your rival."

Amy's chin came up. "Maybe you're jealous, Meg. Ever think of that?"

"Jealous of what?"

"Well, you're not exactly beautiful," Amy said.

"Thanks a lot . . . Think about 'S.' And all the other women Robert Pryce makes a play for. The guy's trouble, you know that."

"I know that I like the way he makes me feel. As if I'm special."

"I think you're making a mistake, Amy. And cut it out. I'd never say a thing like that to you, that you're 'not exactly beautiful.'"

"Well, no, because it wouldn't be true."

"We're supposed to be friends. Friends don't say mean things to each other."

That was our first quarrel, and it took a couple of days to get back to our usual friendliness. Those were a horrible few days. I went around with a great hollow pit in my stomach until we were best friends again. Well, maybe not exactly best friends. Amy had made another friend at school — Louise was her name — and they began to spend a few recesses and lunch hours together.

We didn't find any more notes, but we did notice Sylvia Ballard hanging around that stretch of road. "We could set a trap," suggested Amy. "We could write a note to 'R,' signed 'S.'"

"But then we'd have to copy Mrs. Ballard's handwriting, and we don't know what it looks like."

"You could find out the next time you babysit there. Get a sample, a grocery list or a note, something like that."

Amy turned to me, putting her hand up to her hair. "How do you like it this way?"

"You mean that streak at the front? It looks good. What did you use, peroxide?"

"Yes. I'm thinking of doing the whole thing. My hair is kind of mousey, not really blonde."

"Peroxide is supposed to be bad for your hair," I said. "And you'd have to keep doing it. Otherwise, you'll begin to look like a skunk ... I read somewhere that if you use a lemon rinse after your shampoo, it will bring out all the blonde, brighten it up. Or if you want to go darker, use vinegar."

"I'll try the lemon juice tonight."

I walked her back to her house. For a change, her mother wasn't home. We went down to Amy's bedroom, which was in the shed beneath the front porch. Amy had plastered the walls with pictures cut from movie magazines. She began pointing out all the blonde actresses.

"I wouldn't want to go as light as Alice Faye," she said. "Or Veronica Lake. I like the colour of Lauren Bacall's hair best. It's sort of tawny-coloured. I think I'll start practising her voice. It's so sexy."

We went back upstairs to see if we could find something to eat. There was nothing but peanut butter and crackers, and we took them out onto the front porch. From there we saw my brother Dan, who's four years younger than me, come hurrying up from the wharf. As he got closer, we saw that his clothes were dripping, and his shoulders were hunched up around his ears.

"Hey, Dan!" I called out. "What happened?"

"Nothing," he said and walked away even faster.

"I can get him to tell me," Amy said. "He's got a crush on me."

She left me to go after Dan, and when he spotted her, he began to walk even faster until he was almost running.

Amy turned to come back, but before she did, Mrs. Miller arrived home.

"Don't talk to me," she said, not coming up the steps to the front door but heading around to the back where the bathroom was. "I'm going to have a hot shower and lie down. I don't feel well," she called over her shoulder.

A couple of days later, I asked Dan what had happened. "You looked pretty upset. Did someone push you in the ocean? You were soaked."

"I promised I wouldn't tell," Dan said, turning away.

"Who made you promise?"

"Some jerk guy."

"All the more reason not to keep quiet."

"Well . . . After school, I went down to the wharf to check my cod line, and I heard this shouting from over by Keats Island. It looked like a boat was in trouble. So I took one of the rowboats tied up at the float and rowed across. It was Mrs. Miller and that new guy, you know, the oldest Pryce brother. He said that they'd run out of gas, and he wanted a tow back. That was all right, and I got them here okay, but when I tied up, Mrs. Miller started acting silly, giggling and stuff, and she couldn't get out of the boat. When I tried to help, she fell in between the boat and the float. I bent over to haul her out, but with all her stupid flailing around, she pulled me into the water. Mr. Pryce gave me ten dollars and told me he'd appreciate it if I didn't tell anyone about it . . . The whole thing made me feel kind of sick."

"Did you tell Mom?"

"No. I said I wouldn't tell anyone."

"You told me."

"You don't count."

"Yeah, well, thanks, I love you, too." I told Dan about the notes that Amy and I found.

"I've seen Robert Pryce up in that part of the woods," Dan said. "Yeah, he probably left the notes. I'm not going to have anything more to do with him. The next time he hollers for help, I'm going to pretend I don't hear."

"Dan, do you have a crush on Amy?"

"That's none of your business . . . Maybe I did, once. But one day she said she'd like to climb Lookout Hill with me. Once we got to the top, she told me all these things she wanted me to do with her. I was disgusted. I told Father Smith at confession about it. He explained it all to me and how I'm supposed to resist temptation."

"Dan!"

"I know she's your friend and everything. All I'm saying is that I don't want her coming near me."

I looked at Dan more closely. Dan and sex? I didn't know

whether to believe him or not. But I knew he didn't usually make things up.

As for Amy, had she really tried to seduce him, or was it some kind of a pastime for her, a joke? I decided I would try harder to make friends with the other girls at school.

I was kind of worried about Father Smith, too, about Dan going to confession. Dad was dead set against any of us becoming Catholics. The peninsula had been without a priest as long as we had lived there. Then one was sent from Vancouver to round up all the Catholics and build a church.

"Over my dead body," said my father.

"Murray!" My mother had been raised a Catholic in Ireland, though she hadn't married in the Church, because Dad was a divorced man. "For pity's sake."

A letter came in the mail the next day that took my mind off everything else. Doug Thompson, a soldier that I had been pen pals with, wrote that he was coming home on leave from the Army and that the most important thing to him was that he was finally going to meet me.

Chapter Three

❧

I'D HEARD ALL ABOUT Doug Thompson from his mother, who was a neighbour. She lived two lots over on a wedge-shaped acre whose base was the shoreline. Her husband was away in the Merchant Navy. Before they had built their home there, I used to pick wild strawberries in the meadow and swim in the snug cove. Large rocks at one point of the cove baked hot in the sun and were a perfect place to lie on after a swim.

"Captain Thompson saw the property when he used to work for the Union Steamship Company," Mrs. Thompson told my mother the first day she came to visit. "He said that from the wheelhouse he could see the green meadow among all the cedar trees, and he fell in love with the property. He made inquiries and found that the owner was willing to sell, at a price, and once my husband makes his mind up about anything, that's it. Our son Douglas is the same way. I told my husband that the only way I would live up here was if we kept a small apartment in the city. With him away so much at sea, I didn't want to become completely isolated."

Mrs. Thompson came often to visit Mom, and she usually brought something: scones hot from the oven, a magazine she thought my mother would like to read, a plant cutting from her garden. Not only that, she was generous to me, too.

Once Mrs. Thompson had offered to take me into the city and stay with her in her apartment. "It would be a little holiday for her, Mrs. Woods," she said to my mother, "and she would get to see something of Vancouver."

Mrs. Thompson's apartment was in an old, grey stone building in the West End, and the foyer smelled dusty. We went up the carpeted stairs to her apartment. Once inside, the impression was of droopy plants reminiscent of snakes. The mantelpiece of the small marble fireplace was crowded with photos of her son Douglas: Douglas holding a teddy bear, Douglas with two front teeth missing, Douglas in his Army uniform.

Mrs. Thompson took me to Stanley Park one day and to the art gallery another. After looking at paintings by Emily Carr, we had lunch nearby at the Bay. "It's such a treat to be with a young girl," she said happily, after ordering the day's special for us: grilled cheese sandwiches and mushroom soup. "I've always wanted a daughter. My husband never says much, and Douglas, well, he's like his father in many ways."

She made me feel comfortable. She was like Amy's mother in that way. Both treated me as if they liked me as I was. I could talk to them more easily than to my mother, who always seemed on the alert to teach, or correct, me.

As we were finishing lunch, Mrs. Thompson asked me to write to her son Douglas. I said yes. It was a way for me to contribute to the war effort. At school we knit squares for afghans and rolled balls of foil, but it had all seemed pretty feeble to me.

"Our boys in the services need our letters and support," she said. "It helps their morale. I know that Douglas would like more mail. My husband — being away at sea — doesn't write much, never has. I'm lucky to get a postcard from him."

"What should I write about?"

"Just ordinary things. What you like to read. What's happening with your friends. He's fond of funny stories, so anything humorous. What else? Well, he likes photography, and he's good at drawing."

My letters will be dull, I thought, unless I really work hard to make them interesting. I did write to my oldest brother, Sam, and to my father, both away in the Air Force. But those letters wouldn't suit Douglas.

"We all have to do our bit on the home front," Mrs. Thompson was saying. "It is our duty to write to our servicemen."

"I could send him newspaper clippings and cartoons."

"He'd like that," she said. "Here, I'll write out his address for you. He's taking his basic training at Maple Creek in Saskatchewan."

May 3, 1944

Dear Doug,

I'm going to call you Doug, even though your mother calls you Douglas. Douglas sounds so formal. I hope you don't mind. Your mother said you like to get letters.

Here are a couple of stories I found in the Reader's Digest. The cartoon is from the Vancouver Sun. If you don't think they're funny, tell me, and I won't send any more. I know that everyone has a different sense of humour. My brother, Dan, loves puns, and puns make me cringe. I hope you don't like puns. Hope I haven't offended you.

My best friend's mother lends me books all the time, which is great because there's no library here. She gets them from the Book of the Month Club. They mail a new one to her every month. Right now I'm reading "Kitty Foyle." I think it's interesting that the author, a man, can understand how a woman thinks. Usually, when men write as if they were women, they don't get it right. I haven't read any books where a woman is trying to be a man. I read a lot. Well, not as much as I'd like to.

That's enough about me. Write and tell me what it's like to be stationed in Saskatchewan. Bet you miss the mountains and the ocean.

Your friend,
Meg

He must have written by return mail. I saw the postmaster look at the return address before he handed me the envelope. Amy was with me, and I put the letter in my pocket to read when I got home and was alone in my room. Somehow I didn't want Amy to know.

May 6, 1944

Dear Meg,

Thank you for your letter. I was surprised and pleased to receive it and felt I knew you right away.

To answer your questions:

Here on the base, everyone calls me Doug. Except for the sergeant. He calls me, "Hey, you."

I liked the clippings you sent. I do like puns, though, and you haven't offended me.

I don't read novels, so I haven't read Kitty Foyle. I read the newspaper and Life, and that's about it.

Maple Creek is a little town near Cypress Hills, and I go there on my days off. The people are very friendly, and we get invited to their homes for dinner. I don't have time to miss the mountains and the sea.

You haven't told me what you like to do. I like to dance and go to every dance I can. I like jazz, especially New Orleans, and I've got a record collection that I add to every chance I get. I especially like Muggsy Spanier.

Please write me again soon. I get lonely here.

Your friend,
Doug

P.S. Do you have a snap of yourself?

May 14, 1944

Dear Doug,

Thanks for your letter. I like jazz, too, and dancing. There is a dance here every month, and they play records. I really like Bunny Berigan's "I Can't Get Started With You" and Glenn Miller, of course, his "String of Pearls" and "Moonglow."

My brother, Sam, taught me how to drive last time he was home on leave from the Air Force. He took me up to the North Road where there's almost no traffic. The hardest part was learning how to shift gears. I don't think I ever got it right. He winced a lot.

*You haven't told me much about yourself, so I have
some questions. How old are you? What are you learning
in basic training? What are you going to do after basic
training?*

I hope you write again.

*Your friend,
Meg*

*P.S. I'm sorry, I don't have a snap. Your mother and I
had our picture taken on Granville Street by a street
photographer last month, and she may have the photo.*

When I told my mother I was writing to Doug Thompson,
she said, "I haven't met the young man, but if he is anything
like his mother, he'll be all right." I was surprised. I had
thought she'd say she didn't think it was a good idea, that
Doug was too old for me. As for Mrs. Thompson, she never
said anything to me about the letters.

I finally told Amy about Doug. "Mmmm," she said and
tossed her hair. Things were cooling down between Amy and
me. She'd made this new friend at school, Louise, and had
been going over to her house in Gibson's a couple of times a
week. I missed Amy. Missed our long talks. It was definitely
time for me to try to make more friends.

Doug's last letter worried me. I'd never thought this would
happen. I read his letter again, hoping I'd misread it.

May 23, 1944

Dear Meg,

I've waited to the last minute to let you know my big news. I've finished basic training and am being transferred to the coast for an instructor's course. I haven't told my mother the exact day I arrive, but with the right connections, I should be up on the Friday night boat. That's Friday, June 2.

I'm hoping that you'll be there on the wharf waiting for me. I can't wait to see you, and I don't want anyone else there. I've even started dreaming about you. I can't wait to hold you.

Love,
Doug

How had I ever got into this mess? How was I going to get out of it? All I wanted to do was hide somewhere until he went away.

I talked to Amy about it. She was all for my meeting him.

"You must have led him on, Meg." I started to protest, but she kept talking. "You never know what might happen. Maybe he's really good-looking, and you'll fall for him. Even get married. I know a girl who got married when she was sixteen. Had twins when she was seventeen."

"Really?"

"Yes, he was in the Navy and was going overseas. He was

afraid that he could get injured or killed. This way he would have at least had some happiness first."

"Is he still alive?"

"As far as I know. Do it, meet Doug. I could be your bridesmaid. I'll wear a long bridesmaid's dress. Blue. Blue is my best colour."

May 27, 1944

Dear Doug,

I'm sorry, but I won't be meeting you on the wharf when you arrive.

I don't want a boyfriend yet.

I'm very sorry. I thought we could just be pen pals.

Your friend,
Meg

"Where are you off to at this time of the evening?" my mother called to me as I tried slip out the back door.

"I need to mail an important letter. I want it to go out on tomorrow's boat."

"What important letter is that?"

"To Doug Thompson. He's coming to visit his mother for a few days, and he's got this idea that I should be his girlfriend."

"I'm not surprised. They're Scottish, you know. The Scots are all oversexed."

"How can you say that? You're always telling me not to be prejudiced."

"It's all the oatmeal they eat. It overheats the blood. Anyway, you've plenty of time to have a boyfriend. Here, I have a couple of letters to mail, too. You can take them with you."

There was still orange light in the western sky, and the robins were singing their last songs of the day. The smell of moisture sprang up from the cooling earth. By the time I'd dropped the letters through the mail slot of the general store, the tangerine sky had became tinged with rose and mauve.

On my way home, our dog Pep came bounding out of the woods to greet me. He trotted happily beside me until we were almost at our house. Then he darted into the woods, ran partway up the trail, and began to bark.

I called to him several times, but he ignored me. I heard voices coming from further up the trail. Curious, I found a log set well back on the opposite side of the road and sat on it to wait.

I sat up straighter when I heard a man's angry voice, a woman's *shushing* sounds and a yelp from Pep as if he had been hit or kicked. A few minutes later, Pep came whimpering out of the woods with his tail between his legs. He headed over to me and rested his head on my knee. I stroked him between his ears.

I sat and waited some more. I wasn't scared, only angry that Pep had been hurt. By now, it was almost dark, but not so dark that I didn't recognize the two figures that finally emerged from the woods. I shrank back out of sight.

The first was Robert Pryce. The woman who trailed behind him, adjusting her clothing, was Sylvia Ballard. Robert turned around and said to her, "Sweetie, let me go ahead first. Give me five minutes. It's best that way."

Then I remembered that Robert Pryce called every woman "Sweetie."

Amy and I used to joke about it. "That way he doesn't have to remember their names," we'd agreed.

Not "S" for Sylvia, but "S" for Sweetie.

Chapter Four

❦

I MET THE UNION STEAMSHIP on Friday evening. Their many Lady boats called in at the Landing daily, with an extra sailing on Friday evenings for the weekend visitors. I stood in the shadow just inside the wharf shed, waiting for Doug to come down the gangplank, go up the wharf and disappear. Then I would come out and join the rest of the crowd.

There was no mistaking him. He was the only passenger in uniform who was standing on the deck as the *Lady Cynthia* docked. A young woman stood beside him with her arm tucked under his. It hadn't taken him long to find another girl. He looked directly over my way, as if he had seen me, then turned to the woman and said something. Their laughter floated over the air towards me.

It was impossible to hear what they said, but my imagination went wild: "There's the young kid I thought I'd fallen for." I stepped back further into the shadow of the shed and stayed there until I saw Doug and the woman come down the gangplank and disappear up the wharf.

I needed to talk to Amy. Just as I thought that, Amy appeared at the shed door.

"Why are you hiding in here? Robert Pryce told me that his youngest brother is on the boat. You don't want to miss this. That must be him coming down the gangplank."

"The one in the blue V-neck sweater?" I asked. "He doesn't look much like Robert, or the other Pryce brothers. He's fair, they're all dark." He was taller than the other Pryce men and moved with a certain grace.

"He's seventeen. Name's Glen," Amy said. "Half-brother, really. Different mother. He's been at a private school back east, and they get out earlier than we do. Think you could go for him, Meg?"

"No. I don't like the Pryce men. They're nothing but trouble."

"Well, I think he's cute. But if you're not interested . . ."

"Meaning?"

"I am. He's a Pryce."

By mid-June, the summer visitors began to arrive. The swimming float was brought over from behind Shelter Island, where it had been anchored over the winter. It was tied to a huge log that lay at the back of the swimming beach. A long, narrow, wooden walkway joined the float to the beach.

Rowboats, inboards, and outboards were scraped and painted and tied up at the end of the float. Trim sailboats lay anchored further off. Yachts began to arrive.

One day after picking up the mail, I wandered up to the tennis court to see if its wooden floor had been repaired. It's not that I ever played tennis, but it was something to do other than go home. Amy had arranged to get out of school a week early and had gone into Vancouver to stay with her father for a month, and I was on my own. The summer people had built the court above the creek, a raised wooden platform partially hidden in the cedars. Dances were held there, too. Once Labour Day was over, the court was deserted for the winter.

Someone had been cleaning up around the tennis court. The pathway had been cut back from the encroaching ferns and blackberry bushes. New planks glistened in the floor, as yet unpainted. I closed my eyes, imagining what it would be like to dance with a full moon rising over Keats Island, the whole scene visible through the cedars.

"Hi! Don't let me scare you," a male voice said behind me. My eyes snapped open, and I turned around.

It was the boy I'd seen on the *Lady Cynthia* a few days before, Glen Pryce. The sound of his footsteps must have been muffled by the pine needles on the path. Without thinking, I moved towards the few steps leading down and away from the tennis court. I had to pass him on the path, but he didn't step back to make room.

Instead, he said, "Don't go because of me."

"I was going, anyway." I started to edge past him. A blackberry vine tore at my leg. I could feel the heat radiating from his body.

"Aren't you even going to let me introduce myself? I already know who you are because I asked my brother, Robert. I'm Glen Pryce, and I'm from Ontario."

He reached out his hand and placed it on my arm. It felt too heavy. I brushed it away and kept moving. Fast.

Reaching the bottom of the path, and in clear sight of the road, I called back, "I don't like your brother, Robert, and I don't want to get to know you. So do me a big favour and just leave me alone."

He was down the path in one bounding leap and beside me almost before I knew it. Out of breath, he said, "For such a pretty girl, you're sure a spitfire. I'm not like my brother. I can guess why you don't like him. But why can't you give me a chance? I'm not as bad as you think. We could be friends."

Friends. "Can a boy and a girl just be friends?" I said.

"I've never tried it, but I don't see why not," he said. His eyes were blue and piercing. "Let me walk with you. I'm not going to bite. What exactly did my brother do that put you off?"

I didn't know how to answer, so I just kept on going. Down the path, through the trees to the road and turned left for home.

"You walk fast for a girl," he said, right beside me.

"That's from trying to keep up with my brothers."

"Brothers? How many brothers do you have?"

"Two. Sam is twenty-two. Dan is thirteen."

"I have four brothers. Well, a couple of them are half-brothers. Same father, different mothers."

He stopped walking. I stopped, too, and looked up at him. The sunlight caught in his eyes, and, just like that, I fell for Glen Pryce.

We talked about families and school and our favourite songs, as if we were already friends. I told him about moving to the Landing from Calgary and how lonely I felt leaving all my friends behind. By this time, we'd reached the bridge over the creek that ran by his brother Robert's house.

"This is where I turn down," he said.

I didn't want him to go.

"Wild strawberries grow by the creek," I said. "And water cress."

"Would you like to go out with me sometime?" he said.

Below, the creek murmured as it ran over its bed of mountain stones. A squirrel chattered from a nearby alder. The air was moist and cool on my cheek.

"My mother says I should wait a while before I start to date."

"You don't look too young to me."

"I thought we were going to be just friends."

"Friends can date. Besides, we won't call them dates. We'll

just accidentally meet. Like now. You know, just to talk. Do you play tennis?"

"I've never tried."

"Back home, my father runs a resort hotel, and I've learned to do everything. Had to, to help entertain the guests. I've taught them dancing, tennis, golf ... Do you want to learn how to play tennis?"

"You mean you'd be my teacher?"

"Teacher, friend. When I'm gone, you'll have all these talents, and once you're ready to date, you'll always have as many as you want."

"Dates?"

"Dates. Friends. Both sexes. They're called social skills. It doesn't look as if you have much chance to learn any, living in the backwoods like this."

"What about the summer people? They're not going to like us using their tennis court."

"Wait until I bring all my records to play on their record player at the dances. As long as you're with me, you'll be okay."

Did he mean I'd be going to dances with him?

"So your first tennis lesson is tomorrow morning. Early. Nine o'clock. I'll bring the racquets and balls."

"Okay."

When he smiled, his eyes were even larger, bluer, and more direct. Friend, at the very least, I thought.

Wow.

"You're away early this morning," Mom said to me after I'd done the dishes and was heading out the back door.

"Glen Pryce is going to teach me how to play tennis."

"Another Pryce? I hadn't heard about this one."

"He's the youngest brother. Seventeen. He's visiting from Ontario."

"That's nice," she said, absently. "Would you bring two quarts of milk back with you when you come home? Here, I'll get you the change."

"You need to hold the racquet like this," Glen said, and he took my hand and placed it closer to the end of the racquet. Perspiration broke out on my forehead, even though the morning sun had not yet warmed the air. "The same way you'd hold the handle of a frying pan."

He moved over to the other side of the court and bounced his tennis ball off his racquet a few times. "I'll lob a few over to your side, and you hit them back. Later, when they put the net up, I'll show you how to hit them so that I can't reach them."

The next hour was spent batting balls back and forth to each other. "Let's stop for a break," Glen said. "I saw a water tap down near the end of the path."

After we'd had a drink, he said, "It's cooler down here. Come sit on the log." I sat. "You're nice to be with, Meg. I wish I'd known you before, like all my life. It might have helped."

"Helped what?"

"Being left by my mother. Yeah, when I was three." He began to dig his heel savagely into the layer of pine needles that
cushioned the path. "I hate my father. I hate him! Don't look
so shocked, I have good reason. My father's been married before. My mother was wife number four. When I was three
years old, he kicked my mother out, and I never saw her
again."

"I didn't think fathers could do that."

"Mine did. He's a pretty powerful man."

"How, powerful?"

"Money powerful. He knows the right people."

I thought of my own mother. She would never in a million
years let anyone make her leave a child of hers.

"What did your mother do that was so bad your father
made her leave?"

Glen mumbled something about "another man." His eyes
had dimmed.

"You must have missed her. Miss her. But, Glen, now that
you're grown up, you could always find her and get to know
her."

"He won't tell me where she is."

"Find out some other way," I said.

"I'm trying. One of my father's friends might tell me. He's
a good guy. He helped me out once before . . . It's like I've got
this big hole in me that I can't fill up with anything else, no
matter how I try. Did I tell you I was pretty much an alco-

holic by the time I was fifteen? Plenty of booze around the hotel."

"How did you stop?"

"I'd left home and was living on the streets. Even stole in order to eat. One day, it just hit me that I was going to be dead before I was twenty if I kept drinking. Got a job with a nice guy — the man I mentioned." He pulled out his wallet and showed me a snapshot. "We still keep in touch," he said. "Anyway, when I got on my feet again, I decided to go back to school. That meant living with my father again."

"What grade are you in? You must have lost at least a year."

"No, not that long. I caught up. No trouble. I've got a photographic memory."

We heard the Union Steamship's whistle sound out across the water as she prepared to dock at the Landing: one long, two short, and one long. "It's later than I thought," I said. "The mail will be in soon. I should go."

"How do you like tennis so far?" Glen asked, getting up. He reached down and took my hand to help me stand.

"I like it. You're a good teacher."

"How about swimming lessons?"

"I can swim already, thanks."

"Dancing? I could bring my portable radio to the tennis court one evening."

"Afternoon would be better," I said, thinking of my mother.

"How about today?"

"Okay."

By the time I went back to the tennis court that afternoon, I felt almost giddy with knowing Glen.

"That colour suits you," Glen said, coming towards me. "It makes your eyes look even greener . . . I've found one radio station that plays big band music all day long. Do you know how to dance?"

"My older brother — the one that's away in the Air Force — taught me, but I haven't had much practice lately."

"Let's start with the two-step." He held out his arms. "Let me hold you right for starters. Closer than that. Okay? 'I Can't Get Started With You' is one of my favourites."

Taking my hand, he put it on his shoulder, then put his hand on the small of my back. The trumpet solo filled the air, and the tennis court became a different place, a magical place. We fit together perfectly. Even though he was much taller, my head seemed just right for his shoulder.

By the time the sun began to slide down the western sky, I knew that I'd been away too long and that Mom was going to be furious.

"I'm sorry, Mom," I said, coming in the back door. "I lost track of time."

"Didn't you get hungry? You've never been so late coming home for supper. It's there on the table, but it's cold and dry by now. Where have you been all this time?"

"I was up at the tennis court learning how to dance."

"Who were you with?"

I hesitated. "The summer kids use it for dancing, you know."

"Yes, but the summer people can't usually be bothered with the locals. I hope they weren't playing that darkie music, that jazz, or whatever it's called. It gets people too worked up . . . Come along, don't dawdle. You can clean up the kitchen after you're done . . . I've got some good news for you. Mrs. Hanson at the guest house is looking for help. She's booked up solid for the season, she says. I tell her it's because of her cooking. She wants you for two hours in the morning and two hours in the late afternoon . . . Why the long face? You're the one who wants to stay on in school, and it's up to you to buy your own school clothes and books."

"No, I want the job," I said. Would I still have time to play tennis?

"Meg, you know that you don't really have to go on in school. It's the boys who need the education, not girls. They're the ones who have to be able to find a good job to support their families. You're only going to get married and stay home to take care of the children."

Whenever I heard this, I got furious, and I'd been hearing it all my life. "Yes, well . . . Maybe I'd like to do something more with my life."

How could I explain to her that yearning that made me restless, made me ache to be *someone*. Someone important, special. Not to ever hear again, "You can't do it, have it, even think about it. You're just a girl." What that special thing was

I didn't know. All sorts of impossible ideas came and went: a singer, a writer, a research scientist.

"All I can say, Meagan, is that you've got to face reality. I had to quit in grade four to help out on the farm."

"I know, Mom. You said it was the saddest day of your life."

"Yes, it was." She cleared her throat and spoke briskly. "Enough of that. Mrs. Hanson wants you six days a week. You'll be washing dishes, making beds, doing laundry and helping with the dinner."

Mom picked up her mending basket and fitted a burned-out light bulb into one of Dan's socks. Her needle wove back and forth as she darned. "Oh, and Mrs. Ballard wants you to babysit this Friday at seven. Funny thing about Mrs. Ballard. She and Amy Miller's mother were both in the Co-op at Gibson's this morning when I was there ordering the week's groceries, and neither one spoke to the other. You'd think they had a falling out, or something. What over, I can't imagine. I know that Mr. Ballard is worried about his business, but that shouldn't have anything to do with Mrs. Miller. Oh, well. Maybe he's grouchy at home, and it's spilled over on his wife."

"When does Mrs. Hanson want me to start?"

"On the Thursday before Dominion Day weekend."

Good, I thought. I still had a few free days to play tennis with Glen.

Chapter Five

❦

A HANGING WOODEN SIGN, with the words "Hanson's Guest House," creaked in the brisk ocean breeze. Large, white clamshells lined both sides of the path leading to the front door. I could smell baking bread and freshly brewed coffee. From the open kitchen window came the sound of a radio broadcaster announcing the bombings of London with German V-1 flying bombs, the buzz bombs.

I couldn't help feeling anxious about the war. When the Japanese bombed the ships in Pearl Harbor, I had nightmares for three nights. I dreamed that all the trees around the school were filled with Japanese soldiers holding rifles with bayonets. One week Japanese subs were reported being seen in Georgia Strait, and at night I pulled the bed covers high, almost over my head.

Mrs. Hanson was a good advertisement for her cooking. Plump, rosy-cheeked, with a light dusting of flour up both arms, she wore a white apron over a bright printed house-dress. She had a round face and round blue eyes that seemed to take in everything about me at once. Her manner was pleasant and direct.

"Fifty cents an hour. From nine to eleven each morning and three to five in the afternoon. I'll want you Monday to Saturday, starting this Thursday. We're booked solid for Dominion Day weekend, and I need help to get ready."

The first thing Mrs. Hanson did when I turned up for work on Thursday morning was wrap me in a big, white apron. "There's a sink full of breakfast dishes waiting for you," she said.

After that, it was a frantic rush to make up eight beds with fresh linen. The sheets and pillowcases smelled of sunshine and lavender. I scrubbed bathrooms and stocked them with geranium soap and thick towels. All the silverware had to be cleaned and polished. Then it was out to the garden to clip sweet-smelling roses of pink, red and yellow, to fill vases in the hallways and the large front room that overlooked the wharf.

Mrs. Hanson's daughter helped her with the cooking. Anna was in her twenties, slim, blonde and energetic. She made bread and rolls, pies, puddings and delicate cookies that looked like cones of golden lace.

Everyone was expected to help in the garden, and that included me. "The garden's a godsend," said Mrs. Hanson. "With food rationing and meatless Tuesdays, at least I have plenty of fruit and vegetables to put on the table for the guests. Lucky for me, my sister lives on a farm on the North Road, and she keeps me well supplied with eggs and milk."

Anna and I moved gaily-striped canvas deck chairs from the basement, wiped them off and set them on the front veranda. From the veranda, you could see the government wharf below and west, all the way out the Gap to the Georgia Strait beyond. To the east, the Coast Mountains rose like blue guardians behind Gambier Island. Any time of the day or night, something was happening on the water: sailboats, motorboats, rowboats, canoes, tugboats and the Union Steamship Lady boats. Small boys fished for sea bass from the float. Older boys baited cod lines off the end of the wharf.

As soon as I finished at Mrs. Hanson's for the morning, I hurried to meet Glen at the tennis court. He grinned and said, "You smell good enough to eat."

"Mrs. Hanson and her daughter baked cinnamon buns. I've got a couple for us."

"I've got something important to tell you," he said. His face was bright with excitement. "I've found out where my mother is!"

I stared at him. "What? Already?"

"It's true," he said, his eyes larger than usual. "I thought about what you said about finding my mother." He grabbed my hands. "So I phoned the man who's been a good friend to me — I showed you his picture — and asked him if he knew how I could find her. He said she's kept in touch with him all these years. She wanted to have some way of knowing how I was, and she knew my father wasn't going to tell her."

"And? Where is she now?"

"She's living in Vancouver. Yes, that close. After my father divorced her, she married again, a doctor, and they have two children. She's Mrs. Harold Barras now. My friend gave me her phone number and address. She lives out by the university."

"That's wonderful," I said.

"I talked to her on the phone last night. She was laughing and crying and calling to her husband all at the same time . . . I'm going in on the four o'clock boat today. She invited me to stay with them so we could get to know each other. They're all coming down to meet me when the boat docks in Vancouver at six."

"Do you think you'll recognize her?" I asked.

"I've seen old photos. She says to look for two redheaded kids, twelve and fourteen."

"I still find this hard to believe," I said. "I mean to be leaving so soon! How are you feeling?" I searched his face.

"Scared. Excited. Mostly scared."

I was so happy with his news, I hugged him.

"I'll be back, probably in three or four days. I'll phone you, Meg."

"We don't have a phone," I reminded him.

"I forgot . . . As soon as I get back, I'll leave you a note at Mrs. Hanson's. Wish me luck."

"You know I do."

Later that afternoon, as I was shelling peas for Mrs. Hanson, I heard the *Lady Pam* whistle out on the Sound. I went out on the veranda hoping to see Glen as he left for Vancouver. At last, I spotted him standing on the upper deck, near the wheelhouse. I waved widely until he waved back.

Mrs. Hanson called me in. "Peel these potatoes, please, Meg. After that, you can wash the lettuce and tear it into bite-size pieces. Do you know how to make radish roses? Good."

I was glad of the work. It helped to take my mind off the hollow spot that was back again under my ribs. Amy and Glen, both in Vancouver. Once again, no friends to share with.

On our breaks from playing tennis, Glen and I had talked about what we wanted to do with our lives. I said that I liked writing. "I get A's in composition at school. I love to read. My brothers say I'm nosey. I read somewhere that all good writers are curious."

"I'd like to write, too," said Glen. "I might be a journalist, or something like that. You've got to get the breaks, though."

"First, talent," I said. "That's what I'm not sure I have."

"The main thing is to practise," he said. "Like tennis. Why don't you start by keeping a journal about Mrs. Hanson's Guest House? You could write something every day."

I found an unused school scribbler and began.

Saturday, July 1, 1944

Dear Journal,

We're having a dance at Mrs. Hanson's Guest House tonight. Mrs. Hanson has a huge living room and dining room. Once the furniture is pushed out of the way, there's lots of room. There's a wind-up gramophone and the latest records for the guests. Not that I see anyone who looks particularly interested in dancing. We've got two old spinsters who like to sit on the veranda and look at the scenery and watch the people on the wharf. There's one newly married couple who might be interested, though they seem to spend most of their time in their room. There's another married couple — he's a dentist — with their little boy. I don't know what's going on there. Her mother is with them, and the mother and daughter whisper things about the husband while he tries to do jolly things with the son. I feel sorry for the husband. The two women are against him, and the son acts as if he wishes his father would leave him alone so that he could fish for shiners. I think that couple isn't going to last.

Mrs. Hanson has a son, too. Bruce. He's in the Navy and home on sick leave. He's twenty-two, very good-looking, tall, moves like a dream, but he's not very friendly. Mrs. Hanson says that Bruce was badly burned when his ship was torpedoed in the North Atlantic, and he's had to have skin grafts. Her own husband was killed in a logging accident a long time ago. She started the guest house to make a living. She and Anna dote on Bruce. I've given up trying to get a smile from him. I have to make his bed and keep his room clean, and he never says a word, not even hello. He's an officer, something to do with radar, which is a new discovery. He doesn't seem to have a girlfriend. Maybe that's part of his problem.

One of the spinster sisters, Edith, lost a cameo brooch, and we turned the place upside down looking for it. She said she was given it by her fiancé who was killed in the First World War. I helped her search the room, and I was surprised to see she had brought all of his letters with her. They're tied with ribbons and sorted by years. She went around with pink eyes and a damp handkerchief for hours. I decided I would look under the veranda when I had the time. Maybe the cameo had fallen off her blouse and through the spaced planks that made up the veranda floor. Her sister kept saying, "Now, Edith. Don't carry on so."

July 5, 1944

There's a Bing cherry tree in Mrs. Hanson's side garden,
and she wanted to make cherry pies for dinner tonight. She
asked Bruce to pick the cherries, but he said, "Sorry. Too
much pain. I thought I'd take the boat out." From up the
cherry tree, I watched him stash his fishing tackle in the
back of the putt-putt and head out towards Salmon Rock.
I saw a couple of flashes of silver as salmon jumped.

I found Edith's cameo hidden behind a bedpost. I was vac-
uuming and heard something rattle up the hose and down
into the dust bag. Edith had huge tears in her eyes when she
thanked me.

The newlyweds emerged more often. They went around
looking besotted. Meanwhile, the dentist's voice developed a
note of desperation. I detested his mother-in-law for siding
with the wife, maybe because he was always pleasant to me,
and she wasn't.

I'd be glad when Glen got back. I missed playing tennis
with him. I hadn't heard from Amy, and I had so much to tell
her. I guessed she was having too much fun to write.

July 6, 1944

At least the Hansons are friendly to me; well, Bruce is
softening a bit, but he's not exactly friendly. Mrs. Hanson
told me something today that might help explain it. "He

still has to have another skin graft. He's had more than his share of pain."

Sometimes, Anna Hanson turns on the radio in the kitchen to listen to the news while we prepare the vegetables for dinner. The talk's mostly about the war. Lately, it's about the Russian troops retaking Minsk. I'm glad when the news is over, and we can listen to the music. Number one on the hit parade this week is Frank Sinatra singing, "I'll Be Seeing You." Too bad Frank Sinatra's so skinny. Glen's not. They play Duke Ellington's "Don't Get Around Much Anymore" on the radio a lot. It makes me feel like dancing. Today, I tried a few steps of jitterbug in the kitchen, and Bruce came in while I was dancing. He was dangling two coho through the gills, one on each forefinger. He stared at me for a minute and said, "You're not a bad dancer." For some insane reason, I winked at him and then, mortified at what I'd done, bolted out the back door.

Chapter Six

❧

MY FATHER CAME HOME unexpectedly on a few days' leave from the Air Force. He was on his way to the Queen Charlotte Islands to run the power station at Alliford Bay.

One morning while we were all still eating breakfast, the priest, Father Smith, called in at our house. He refused the coffee my mother offered.

"I have other things on my mind," he said to Mom, but looking at Dad. "I'll get right to the point. In the eyes of the Holy Church, you two are not married. You are committing a sin if you persist in having a physical relationship."

"Not married? What kind of crazy talk is this?" said Dad, standing up and pushing his chair back.

"Because you are a divorced man, Mr. Woods. The Church does not recognize this marriage. The only way you can continue to stay together is if you live as brother and sister."

Dad reached over and took Father Smith by the scruff of his neck and hustled him out the back door.

"You damned excuse for a man," he yelled. "Get out of here. And don't come back. How dare you interfere between a man and his wife? If I ever catch you around here again, I'll beat the living daylights out of you."

I watched from the window as Father Smith started to crank his old Chev. His face got redder and redder. Finally the engine caught, and he jumped into the front seat and left in a black cloud of burning oil.

Mom was crying and trying to hush Dad at the same time.

Whenever my parents fought, I found it better to leave and stay away as long as possible until things cooled down. That's what I did, wishing that I could talk to Amy. She was still in Vancouver. I went down to the beach and skipped stones across the water for the next half-hour.

The next morning, there was a note for me from Glen at Mrs. Hanson's. *Back from Vancouver. Have to see you. Will be waiting for you when you get off work. Glen XOX*

I wondered if Mrs. Hanson or her daughter Anna had read the note. They must have because as I got ready to leave at eleven, Anna handed me two small brown paper bags, the kind the guest house packed for those who wanted a picnic lunch. Anna winked. Whoops. Had Bruce told them that I had winked at him?

Glen was waiting for me outside Mrs. Hanson's back gate. I had forgotten how handsome he was. We took the path down to the beach. Finding a warm spot in the sun, we propped ourselves against a log. The tide was out, and the sand lay glistening before us.

"Tell me everything," I said. "Start with your mother."

"I'm still trying to sort things out," he said. "My mother's husband seems okay, though I don't think he's overjoyed to have me join his family. Can't blame him. My half-sister and half-brother are kind of bratty and want to hang around me all the time ... It's what I thought I wanted, but ... I don't know. I don't feel comfortable." Then he dropped his voice so that I could barely hear him. "I still feel empty."

"Oh, Glen."

He took a deep breath. "They want me to come live with them in Vancouver. Go to university there in the fall."

"I thought you were only seventeen."

"I am, but I finished grade twelve, and I have university entrance. We've already been out to see the campus."

"Then you've decided to go?" I said.

"Not really ... I'd have my own room. They've got this huge house ... My own father will be furious. Probably cut me off financially. But my mother says I can count on her for cash, that she has money of her own."

I couldn't help wondering if Glen could count on his mother. I'd asked him once if she had ever tried to get in touch with him after she'd left him when he was so young, and he'd said no. "I blame my father totally for her absence in my life," he'd said. Again I thought of my own mother. Nothing would have stopped her from getting in touch with a child of hers.

More to hide my feelings than from hunger, I opened the lunch bags and handed Glen a devilled egg sandwich. "Your mother ... What's she like? Do you like her?"

"She's my mother ... I need her, but ... Oh, Meg, I don't know. She's falling all over herself to please me. Maybe she feels guilty. The others don't like it."

The waves made small slapping sounds at the shoreline.

"I'm glad you're back, Glen. It's good to have a friend."

"I missed you," he said, "even though they kept me so darn busy all the time, I hardly had time to think."

"Will you stay here for the summer?" I asked.

"Yeah. I'll go in to see my mother a couple of times before I go into Vancouver for university." He picked up my hand. "I want you to go to the dance with me on Friday night."

"I don't know. My mother's got a thing against dancing. She met my father at a dance and, well ... He swept her off her feet, she says, and has been unfaithful to her ever since."

"Has he?"

"Well ... Maybe. Probably."

"Parents," said Glen, shaking his head. "Don't you wish they'd just behave themselves and let us get on with our own lives?"

Mom was working in the small garden at the front of our house. I knelt down to help her pull weeds. "Anna Hanson is going to the dance tomorrow night at the tennis court," I said, knocking the dirt from a long dandelion root against a stone. "I'd like to go, too."

"How late would you be getting in?"

"I'm not sure when the dance ends. Midnight? I'd come straight home."

She put down the trowel. "You're so young." She stood up and stretched, putting her hand to the small of her back. "Don't be in a hurry to grow up, Meg. It happens fast enough as it is. You know what I think about dancing. I sometimes wonder how my life would be if I'd never gone to that dance where I met your father."

What if Dad were in earshot? They must be still quarrelling, I thought.

Just then Dad spoke from the top of the front doorsteps. "Let the girl go and enjoy herself, Vera," he said. "Don't let the priest turn you sour on our children."

The same old bickering. With Dad away in the Air Force, there had been a break from that. But at least I was going to the dance. I could hardly believe it had been so easy.

"Mom says it's okay for me to go to the dance tomorrow night," I told Glen when he met me after work later that day. "Dad's home, and he stood up for me. But I'd like to meet you at the bridge tomorrow evening, okay? Don't come to my house. My parents are having a bit of a tiff, and I don't want you to see it. Oh, and I have to be home right after the dance."

He leaned forward, as if he were about to kiss me. I didn't move away. He looked at me with those piercing eyes that made me feel as if he knew everything about me and liked it. After a moment, he drew back.

I had nothing to wear to the dance. Finally, I thought of asking Amy's mother. She had always been helpful to me. Once she'd given me a dark red cardigan sweater, saying, "The colour doesn't suit me, and Amy doesn't want it. I think it will look good on you with your dark hair."

The next day I went to see Mrs. Miller, but she didn't answer my knock. I had turned away and was already halfway out the gate when I heard the door open behind me. Looking back, I saw Rob Pryce lounging in the doorway.

"Who is it?" I heard Mrs. Miller's voice call from behind him.

"It's okay, Sweetie," said Rob. "Whoever it was has gone."

"Sweetie" for Sylvia Ballard in the woods and "Sweetie" for Mrs. Miller in her home? I definitely did not like Robert Pryce.

Later that same morning, I knocked again on Mrs. Miller's door. She opened it. No sign of Robert this time. She seemed happy to see me.

"Come in," she said. "I've missed seeing you since Amy's been away in the city."

"I'll be glad when she gets back."

I told her about the dance.

"You really should wear a dress," Mrs. Miller said. "Or a pretty skirt and blouse."

"I don't have any," I said.

"Are you sure?"

"Just ones for school."

"Well, all right, come on in to the bedroom, and I'll see what I can find."

"This is really nice of you, Mrs. Miller."

"No, I'm glad to help." She began to rummage through her closet. "I have a couple in mind. Try this one on ... That colour's not good on you. This one is better, but it's too tight across the bust ... Now, how about this yellow one?"

A yellow dress of polished cotton with printed angel faces drawn in thin black lines, like pencil drawings, it had a tiny bow of the same material at each shoulder. The skirt was full, and the dress fit as if it had been made for me. It was not one I would ever have picked out to wear, but once on, I could see that it was perfect.

Glen was already at the bridge that evening when I got there. His eyes lit up, and I smoothed out the fullness of the skirt. The look in Glen's eyes made up for the disapproving one I'd seen in my mother's when I told her where I'd got the dress.

"Neither a borrower nor a lender be," she'd said.

"You look beautiful," Glen said. "I can't wait to show you off. I want to keep you all to myself, though." The creek murmured under the bridge.

We walked up to the tennis court. The moon, full just two nights before, showed a small bite out of the front curve. I could see its image shimmering on the surface of the ocean spread out below the cedars.

Three or four couples were already waltzing on the dance floor. Anna and Bruce Hanson were one. They danced together so well that I thought they must have practised together, growing up in the same household.

Summer kids began to arrive. The boys had their hair slicked back with Brylcreem, and the girls all smelled of Johnson's baby powder. They were a clique of their own and didn't mix with the locals. They even dressed alike: the boys wore cords and pullover sweaters; the girls wore slacks and long V-necked sweaters that they had knit themselves. I'd seen the girls on the porch of the village store, knitting needles flashing in the sun and balls of brightly coloured yarn poking from the top of patterned cotton bags.

Glen held out his arms to me, and we moved out onto the dance floor. The moon followed us as we danced. The lessons paid off — we knew each other's moves — there were no missteps or awkward turns. Glenn Miller, Tommy Dorsey, Count Basie . . . It was as if their music was being played just for us.

The music was in sets of three. "Stardust" opened the next set, Artie Shaw's clarinet solo rising clear and pure. It was one of my favourites.

Bruce Hanson appeared beside us. "May I cut in?" he said.

Glen's arm tightened around me for a moment, but he dropped both arms and stepped aside.

To dance with Bruce was very different than with Glen. Where Glen's movements were smooth and light, even when holding me close, Bruce held me more at a distance. Maybe his skin grafts were hurting him, I thought. With his hand putting pressure on my back, first this way and then that, we circled the dance floor and ended in the middle. I felt as if I wasn't getting enough air, as if I had been taken over, almost commanded. I was definitely dancing with an older man. It was exciting but a little frightening.

Glenn Miller's "Chattanooga Choo Choo" followed "Little Brown Jug." Bruce started to jitterbug. For the first time, he spoke to me.

"You know how to do this," he said.

I did. All I had to do was follow his lead. He knew exactly what he was doing.

Soon other couples stopped dancing and stood to watch us. Duke Ellington's "Missed the Saturday Dance" began to play, and Johnny Hodges' alto sax led into the melody. Bruce's grip tightened. I wondered where Glen was.

I saw him dancing with Anna Hanson. When the Duke Ellington record finished, Glen came over and cut in on Bruce. I didn't know if I was relieved or not.

"It's good to have you back," he said, as he danced me away from Bruce.

Around eleven, Glen wanted to leave.

"I want to have some time alone with you," he whispered into my ear.

We stopped at the bridge on the way home, leaned over the railing and listened to the water running below. Glen put his arm around my waist and turned me so that we were face to face. His eyes were brilliant in the moonlight.

"I like having you as a friend," he said. "But I want more. To see that Hanson guy dancing with you . . . I didn't like that."

"Glen, I'm —"

"I need you, Meg. You make up for everything."

"I *am* here for you. You know that."

"No, more than that. I want you to belong to me."

He tightened his arms and began to kiss me. It was not the kind of kiss I had always imagined, romantic, loving. It felt too hard, too rough.

I leaned back.

He pulled me in even tighter. The moonlight caught his face at an angle, and at that moment, he looked exactly like his brother, Robert Pryce. I stiffened. He began to kiss me again, more fiercely, and I felt his hand start at the bottom of my skirt and move quickly up my inner leg.

"No!" I said, pushing away.

He grabbed me back. "Wait, wait! We don't have to go all the way. Let me touch you. Here, feel this." He put my hand on the front of him. "I have needs. You do, too."

I struggled and managed to get free. I hurried away. As soon as I got around the bend in the road, I started running towards home.

There were no lights on at my house. I opened the back door and saw my mother standing in the middle of the kitchen floor in a square of moonlight.

"I got up to get a drink of water," she said, "and I saw this patch of moonlight. It was so beautiful, I had to dance in it."

For a second, I saw Mom differently. I thought she would probably understand how upset I felt if I told her what had happened. But she seemed so happy, I didn't want to break the spell for her.

Chapter Seven

❦

MY BOTTOM-RIGHT MOLAR had been acting up for the past month, and now it started to ache with a vengeance. Dad said that I should see a dentist.

"It's too bad there's not one here on the peninsula," he said. "You could come into Vancouver with me on the Sunday-night boat and see the dentist early Monday. I'll get you a room at the Castle Hotel. You can have the tooth attended to on Monday and catch the nine o'clock boat back home Tuesday morning."

"What about work?" I said. "I'm supposed to be helping Mrs. Hanson at the guest house."

Dad shrugged. "Tell Mrs. Hanson about the tooth. She can do without you for that short a time."

"This won't hurt a bit," the dentist said, adjusting the mirror strapped on his head. "We'll have this taken care of in no time."

After it was over, Dad gave me five dollars to go shopping. I added it to the money I had already earned working. I spent 57 cents on a feather cut at the beauty salon at the Bay. The Bay was having their July sales, and I found a tailored shark-skin blouse for $2.95, a straight-cut skirt of cotton twill with a white background and huge, multi-shaded red roses for $3.99, and for $2.99, a short-sleeved sweater the same colour as one of the shades in the roses. With the change left over, I bought a pair of huaraches sandals in a neutral colour.

Dad and I had dinner at Scott's Café, a few steps north on Granville from the hotel. He ordered breaded veal cutlets for two. "The best in Vancouver," he said. "The top chefs of the city come here to eat on their days off."

I seldom had Dad's full attention, and that made it special. I wore my new skirt, blouse and short-sleeved sweater. I felt eyes follow its bright colour as Dad and I made our way to a back booth.

"Tell me about Father Smith," Dad said casually, as he broke open a roll and buttered it. "Does he come around to the house often?"

"Quite a bit," I said. "He's trying to start a new parish. The more Catholics, and those who've been Catholic, that he can round up, the happier Archbishop Duke will be."

"And what do you think of the good priest? Do you like him?"

"He's okay. He doesn't like me, though."

"Oh? Why's that?"

"All I know is that I overheard him tell Father Quinn that I was a lost cause."

"Who's Father Quinn?"

"He's a priest who's visiting Father Smith for the summer. Father Smith's Chevy had a flat tire last week, and both of them came into Mrs. Hanson's to use her phone. Father Smith saw me working in the kitchen, and I heard him say to Father Quinn that he didn't like my attitude."

"Did he, now? Are you sure?"

"He's deaf and he shouts, so, yes, I'm sure."

That was something else I didn't like about Father Smith. When he took confessions, he shouted because of his deafness, and everyone waiting to give confession could hear what he said.

Things like, "That's self-abuse and a sin. Now you are to say ten Our Fathers and fifteen Hail Marys and don't indulge in the habit again."

Dad continued, all the while drumming his fingers on the tabletop. "What else about Father Smith? How does he act when he's visiting the house?"

"Well, he likes Dan. He's 'taking an interest,' he says. Always doing nice things for him."

"What sort of nice things?"

"He gave Dan an old bugle that should have gone to the Sechelt Indian Band. He told Dan that every time he had bad thoughts, he should play the bugle instead. Dan's getting quite good at it."

"And your mother. What sort of things does he say to her?"

"Nothing special. I just know that he leaves a bunch of stuff for us to read. That's probably why he doesn't like me. He enrolled me in a correspondence catechism course taught by the nuns in Edmonton. Mom kept after me to do the lessons. I did one and quit. When Father Smith asked me about it, I told him it was too boring. I said that I didn't like being made to feel guilty all the time. If God made us, He should understand that a person can't always be good, no matter how hard they try."

"The good priest wouldn't have liked that."

"No, he didn't . . . Dad, I've met this really interesting boy. He likes me all right. But, I don't . . ."

"Don't want to go as far as he wants," Dad supplied. "And you shouldn't. There are plenty of other girls around who will give him what he wants. Say no. In the long run, he'll respect you for it. Boys don't marry the easy ones."

"I really am not thinking of getting married. But I'd like us to be friends."

"Friends first, okay. But you need to look ahead. You'll be getting married one of these days." He rearranged the salt and pepper shakers and cleared his throat. "Boys will be boys. I was one once, myself. All I'm saying is not to give yourself away. I promise you that you'll never regret that decision."

I felt strange talking to Dad about this. But he was a man, and I wanted to learn more about how men thought.

Later, I thought about what Dad said. He'd left out the most important reason for not giving a boy what he wanted. Pregnancy. I was determined to a least finish high school and even further, if I could. Pregnancy would cancel all chances for that.

My first day back at Mrs. Hanson's was hectic. The old guests were leaving, and all the rooms had to be cleaned and the beds made up fresh again for the new ones coming on the noon boat. The washing machine in the basement was kept running all morning as load after load of bed linen was washed and then hung out to dry in the sunshine.

Edith gave me a two-dollar tip when she said goodbye. "For finding my cameo," she said. "You know, next to my fiancé's letters, that cameo is the most precious thing in the world to me. You are a dear."

Mrs. Hanson had me set out tea, coffee, cheese, fruit and biscuits in the sunroom for the departing guests. Checkout time was 11:00 a.m., and they had four hours before the Union Steamship returned to the Landing on its way back to Vancouver.

All rooms had been booked. "We have a married couple celebrating their fiftieth wedding anniversary, two university professors, and a family of six from the Cariboo," Mrs. Hanson told me, stacking my arms with fresh linen. "We had another call just the other day from a Vancouver family who wanted to book rooms, but I had to say no. The woman was quite insistent, but I don't have any suitable rooms available.

It was all very last minute — some sort of family thing, I gathered. I told her I was booked up solid until Labour Day. 'People book ahead a year,' I said. I didn't much like her anyway. A bit pushy, I thought. Meg, as soon as you've finished with the rooms, you can start to make the salad. We're going to have a hungry bunch come off the boat at noon, and they'll be looking for their lunch."

As I was washing the lettuce, tomatoes, cucumbers and green onions for the salad, Bruce came into the kitchen. I wondered if he would talk more to me now that we'd danced together.

"I'd like a glass of water," he said to me, leaning against the counter.

My mother would have said, "What about a 'please?'" Or, "Why don't you get your own glass of water?"

But he was my boss's son, and I didn't say anything, just ran the water, filled a glass and handed it to him. His shirt, unbuttoned at the top, gaped. I saw pink, healing flesh across his chest.

"The pain has changed him," Mrs. Hanson had said. "He's not the same. He's angry a lot of the time."

Bruce saw me looking at his exposed chest. He turned away. When he faced me again, his shirt was buttoned.

He finished the glass of water. "You're not a bad dancer," he said, setting the glass on the counter beside the sink.

"I like to dance."

"You've had lessons, I think." He didn't seem to be in any hurry to go anywhere.

"A few."

"Don't say much, do you?" He smiled.

"No."

"But you like to have the last word."

"Always."

"Hmmm. Well, you're a natural when it comes to dancing . . . How old are you, anyway?"

"Seventeen."

Mrs. Hanson came into the kitchen, her face flushed and her eyes bright with tears. "I've just had a phone call from the brother-in-law of the family from the Cariboo who were going to be our guests. The whole family was killed in a head-on collision with a semi on the highway last evening. Dead. All of them. Four beautiful children. Merciful heavens! The parents came here originally on their honeymoon, twelve years ago. I've known those children from the time they were little."

Bruce made a movement to comfort his mother.

She wiped her eyes with the hem of her apron. "I'll phone that Vancouver family and tell them they can come on tomorrow's boat, that there's been an unexpected cancellation."

The next day the Vancouver family arrived. I showed them to their rooms. As I was about to leave, I heard the woman say, "Harold, as soon as we're settled, I'll phone the Pryces and let them know we're here. Mrs. Pryce is still insisting that we stay with them. But she's had TB, Glen tells me, and I'm not going to expose our children to any infection."

"I told you I didn't want to come here," the man grumbled. "But I guess we had to, for our own protection, that is, if you insist we take the boy. I don't want that ex-husband of yours saying I had interfered with his son without his permission. I'm still not one hundred percent convinced it's a good idea . . ." He turned impatiently to me. "Yes, did you want something?"

"The bathroom's at the end of the hall," I said quickly and left.

Should I tell Glen what I'd heard? I spent too much time wondering about that question. We hadn't seen each other since the night on the bridge. Finally, I decided I had to tell him. That's what friends did, looked out for each other, and I wanted at least to be his friend.

I had never been to the Pryce house before. People said that the Pryces didn't encourage visitors. Their German shepherd started barking as soon I opened the gate. From the direction of the beach in front of the house, I heard the sounds of a cornet. Glen had told me he played one, and I followed the notes through the blackberry bushes and down to the ocean.

Glen was sitting on a log, eyes closed, cradling the instrument as if it were a lover. He was playing "Memories of You." The music caused a sweet ache to begin in my chest. I stayed where I was, wanting to hear it through to the end. After he finished, he stood up and shook out the cornet. Drops of saliva glistened in the sunlight. He saw me and came over.

"I've got some news, Glen." I told him about Mrs. Hanson's new guests. "I thought they must be your mother and her husband. The two kids with them are about the right age, too, and they're definitely redheads."

"They'd talked about visiting Rob and getting his okay on me moving into Vancouver with them. They never phoned me that they were coming, though."

"You don't sound overjoyed."

"It's caught me off guard."

"I hate to tell you this, Glen, but your mother's husband doesn't sound too happy about you coming to live with them." I paused. "I didn't know whether to tell you that or not."

"I'm glad you did. I don't want to go there if Harold doesn't want me ... What do you think, Meg?" he asked, a frown between his eyebrows.

"I think you should get to know them better before you move in. University doesn't start for two months. You'll have time to see things more clearly by then."

"Yeah, yeah ... Look, about the other night. I'm sorry. I shouldn't have rushed you like that."

The Barras family was away from the guest house most of the time. Cleaning their rooms each morning, I saw that Dr. Barras liked reading biographies and that she used Max Factor Rose Red lipstick. As for the kids, they read comic books and collected shells and left their clothes on the floor. None of this was worth reporting to Glen.

Mrs. Hanson let the odd comment drop. First it was, "The Barrases are visiting their relatives this afternoon." Next she said, "They climbed Lookout Hill this morning." Later, "They've rented an outboard and tackle to go fishing."

One morning after I'd finished my two-hour morning stint, I met Glen outside the post office. "How's the visit going?" I said. "Do your sister-in-law and your brother like your mother and her husband?"

"Seem to. They're over for drinks every evening, and everyone seems to get along okay. I notice that Harold doesn't like my brother ogling my mother, though. Makes him grumpy."

"He's grumpy at Mrs. Hanson's. Doesn't say much, but goes around looking mad all the time. His patients mustn't like that. What kind of a doctor is he, anyway?"

"A proctologist. Diseases of the rectum."

"Oh . . ." That would explain a lot. I'd feel cranky, too, if I specialized in that part of the human body. Now if he were a brain surgeon . . . "Does your mother get upset when Harold grouses?"

"It's hard for me to know what she thinks. Like about me going to live with her. Is it a guilt trip or something? Does she really want to get to know me, to make up for lost time, as she says?"

"They'll be leaving in a couple of days. Maybe you'll know by then, Glen."

"Another thing," he went on. "Their kids don't like to see their mother paying so much attention to me."

"What makes you say that?"

"They told me, the little buggers. They said it was okay for me to visit once in a while, but they don't want me to come live with them."

"That's nice, isn't it."

"Yeah, but I can't blame them. Oh, and Harold wants me to get a job this summer caddying at the University Golf Club. He says I can't expect him to give me an allowance."

"Does your mother know about all this?"

"I doubt it. They're all careful to say these things when she's out of earshot . . . One thing about their visit is that I'm not getting to see you as often as I'd like. Anyway, you and I are going to the dance together this Friday night, right? I'm not going to let them take up all my time."

"Okay." I'd been hoping he'd ask, though I hadn't forgotten how he'd acted on the bridge. For one thing, I had all these new clothes to wear. But it was a hard line walking between friendship with Glen and his wanting more. I was beginning to doubt if it could work. Perhaps you couldn't just be friends with a boy. Well, I was going to try, anyway.

"Friday's too long to wait to be with you," Glen said. "Rob said I could use his rowboat tomorrow afternoon. Would you like to go over to Shelter Island? The cove there's supposed to be perfect for swimming, and the tide will be high."

It was only half-an-hour's row from the Landing to Shelter Island. We pulled the boat up above the tide line. The sand in the cove was fine and white under our feet.

"No one will bother us here," Glen said, spreading out the

blanket he'd brought. "I want you all to myself today." He stripped to his bathing suit and lay on his back with a sigh. "What a relief not to pretend. I'm tired being on my best be-haviour all the time. The only time I really feel all right is when I'm with you."

I looked at the ocean. I was hot and sweaty from the sun. "I'm going in for a swim." I peeled off my clothes down to my bathing suit.

The water was perfect, cool enough to be refreshing but warm enough to stay in for as long as I wanted. When I had enough, I swam into shore and lay on the blanket next to Glen. He seemed to be asleep.

There were no sounds except for the cries of seagulls and the gentle sigh of waves at the shoreline. What bliss. I lay on my stomach, cradled my head on my hands and closed my eyes.

I woke to find something nudging the side of my thigh. It was warm and hard and unlike anything I'd ever felt before. I raised up on my elbow and looked back.

I was so astonished to see Glen naked in all his glory that I leaped up, grabbed my clothes and ran to the rowboat. I shoved it down into the water and pushed it away from the shore. Clambering into it, I rowed away as fast as I could. Once I was a safe distance away, I yelled back, "You bastard!"

Glen was waving his arms wildly at me. "Come back!" he called. "You can't leave me here!"

I didn't stop rowing. "I'll tell someone to pick you up," I

shouted. "You're lucky I don't leave you to swim back on your own."

Even when I was a good distance from the shore, I could hear him still making a commotion.

An inboard came alongside of me and cut its speed to idle. It was Bruce. "Did you just do what I think you did?" he said.

"What's that?" I pulled even harder on the oars.

"You left your boyfriend behind on the island."

"He's not my boyfriend. Besides, once I've tied up at the float, I'll tell his brother to go get him."

Bruce put the engine into neutral and coasted alongside. "Do you need any help?"

"No, thanks."

"You want me to just leave you alone?"

"Yes, please."

"Well, I'm not going to," he said. "Tie up behind me, and I'll take you in."

"No, thanks. I'm fine."

He didn't seem to hear me. He tied my boat to his, started the engine, opened the throttle and headed for the government wharf.

Chapter Eight

❧

AFTER WASHING AND IRONING the dress I'd borrowed from Mrs. Miller, I returned it. "It was just right, Mrs. Miller. Thank you."

"You're welcome, Meg. I've got good news for you. Amy is coming home this evening."

I was down at the wharf as the *Lady Alexandra* blew its whistle for the Landing. Amy hadn't written me during the four weeks she'd been away. I had hoped she would but told myself she was too busy and excited at being in Vancouver to bother. If we hadn't been the only two girls living in the Landing, would she want to be friends with me at all?

As I watched her come down the gangplank, I thought she

looked more beautiful than ever. She held herself with such assurance. Not like me. I made a conscious effort to stand up straighter. In the long, slanting rays of the setting sun, Amy's hair lay on her shoulders like a cape of burnished gold. She wore more eye makeup than usual, but not so much that she looked cheap, just enough to make her eyes flash in her lightly tanned face. Dressed all in white, she drew everyone's eyes as she stepped down from the gangplank onto the wharf.

I was at her side immediately. "Let me help," I said, taking her suitcase. "Oh, Amy, I missed you so much!"

She talked about her adventures in Vancouver all the way up the wharf. At the head of the wharf, we met Robert Pryce and Glen. "I was beginning to wonder if you'd ever come back," Robert Pryce said to Amy. "Your mother sent me to help carry your suitcase." He took it from my hand.

He introduced Amy to Glen. "I've told you about Amy's mother," he said. What? I felt Amy stiffen beside me.

I had wondered how Glen would act the next time we met and had rehearsed what I would say to him. He completely ignored me and stood staring at Amy Miller. His mouth went slack as his eyes travelled down her body.

I turned to leave. I heard Amy say, "Rob, you and Glen go ahead with my suitcase to my house. I haven't seen Meg for weeks. She's my best friend, and I need to talk to her."

Best friend. She said best friend.

"I've got lots to tell you," Amy said, taking my arm. "I missed you, too! Hey, I thought you'd have more of a tan."

"I've been working at Mrs. Hanson's, so I haven't had that much time . . . Let's go sit under the bridge." It was one of our favourite spots to talk when we didn't want anyone to overhear us. I decided not to say anything to Amy about Glen.

The day still held some light, but it was darker under the bridge, dark enough that it was hard to read Amy's face. I usually took my clues from her. Were her eyes bored? Did she look restless? If so, I would change the subject to one I thought would please her. Usually, it was about her.

"Anything new about Robert Pryce and Mrs. Ballard?" Amy asked, once we had settled ourselves comfortably. The damp air smelled of clean creek water, ferns and alder trees. A car rumbled across the bridge over our heads.

"No. Though Mrs. Ballard has been acting miserable about something. No one knows why. She looks kind of sick to me, all pale and thin."

"Has Robert Pryce been hanging around my house much?" Amy asked in an off-hand way.

"I've been so busy working that I haven't noticed," I said.

"Well, my dad is plenty mad about it. I don't think he's going to come home anymore."

I sat bolt-upright with shock. "You mean, ever?"

"That's what it sounds like. He's talking about a divorce."

I didn't know any divorced people, well, except for Dad and Glen's mother. And Dad and Mom had married long before I was born. People separated, or lived together with someone else, but they didn't divorce. There was a stigma even about the word. Adultery had to be proved. Some men hired a woman to be caught with them in a hotel room, had someone photograph the two of them together, and that was legal grounds for divorce. That's the way it was, even if the wife had been the unfaithful one. It was considered gentlemanly of the husband to protect his wife's name. The whole procedure was expensive, and people on the peninsula often didn't bother. They just went about their business quietly, and others looked the other way.

Amy said, "Even if he doesn't get a divorce, he is not coming back. He'll send money home, and I'll still live here and go to school at Gibson's, but it means that I'll have to go into the city if I want to see him."

"Will you mind that?"

"Not really. I sleep on the couch in the living room of his apartment, and we go lots of places together. I can't wait to show you all the new clothes he bought me . . . This brother of Robert's . . . What's he like? Is there something going on between the two of you?"

"Why makes you ask that?" I said.

"I thought I picked up something, especially on his part. When he looks at you, he gets all tensed up, almost as if he's mad about something."

"Yeah, well, he made a pass, and I didn't like it."

"Oh. So the field's clear then. I wouldn't mind if he made a pass at me. God, the way he's built." Amy sighed deeply.

"He plays tennis. It must be because of that. Come on, let's go. The mosquitoes are eating me up."

"Are you going to the dance tonight, Meg?" Anna Hanson said, as she came into the kitchen the next morning. I rinsed the new potatoes I'd been scraping and put them in a pot of cold water.

"I was going to, but I changed my mind."

"Don't do that," she said. "Bruce needs a partner, and I've got a date with Alfred Kallio tonight. He's an old flame, and I'll be dancing with him all evening. I don't plan to let him slip through my fingers again. Twenty-five and I'm an old maid."

Bruce had come into the room as we were talking. He poured himself a cup of coffee and looked over at me. I never knew what he thought of me. Sometimes he seemed to like me. Like now.

Twenty-five was old to be single all right, but I couldn't help out Anna. "I'm really sorry," I said to her, "but I've picked up another job, a *Vancouver Sun* paper route. The *Tymac* doesn't bring the papers from Horseshoe Bay until around seven, and then I have to deliver them. That will make it too late for me to go to the dance."

"Bruce, you can work something out," Anna said over her shoulder, as she left the kitchen.

"Why are you working so hard?" Bruce said. "You're here twice a day. And now you have a paper route, too? How much money can you make at that?"

"Thirty cents for every dollar paper I sell. I've got twenty-four customers taking the weekend edition. It works out to

$7.20 a week. I've got to work if I want to stay in school. My mother wants me to quit. She says I'm only going to get married anyway and have children. She thinks that only boys need an education. They have to support a wife and family."

"And? What do you think?"

"I know I don't want to end up married with a bunch of children and stuck here in the boonies. I want out." I took a bowl of eggs from the fridge to hard-boil for the potato salad.

"What do you want to do when you're 'out'?"

"I'd really like to go to university. It would mean working for a year first to earn enough to pay for tuition, room and board."

"Have you looked into scholarships for high school students who want to go on to university?" Bruce said.

"I asked my high school teacher, but all the scholarships are for boys. 'Boys only.' That's right. It's what my mother says, too. Boys need the education. It makes me furious."

"Meg, a girl like you has a future ahead of her. You can do anything you want if you make your mind up to it."

"I don't know about that."

"I believe in you, Meg," he said. He took my hand.

The clock ticked loudly in the room, even though, to me, time seemed to have stopped. After a moment, Bruce dropped my hand, and my heartbeat returned to normal.

"I'll tell you what is going to happen tonight," he said. "I'll help you deliver your papers, and we'll go to the dance together. I can't stand by and see a kid like you work all the time, without having some fun. We'll stay at the dance for an hour, and then I'll drive you home. You're working tomorrow, and you need to get your sleep."

Kid. Kid. Kid. "No, thanks."

"Meg, yes," he said. "We'll do it my way."

"I appreciate the thought, but I don't like it when you boss me around. And I'm not a child."

He laughed, and I realized it was the first time I'd heard him laugh. I couldn't help but laugh back.

"I don't think of you as a child," he said. "Not at all. You are a very special young woman. For now, no more arguing."

The guest house owned a 1940 Ford pickup truck, and Bruce drove it down to the foot of the wharf to wait for the *Tymac*. The speedboat was on time, and as soon as the bundle of newspapers was thrown onto the float, I grabbed it by the rope binding the papers, ran up the ramp to the wharf and threw it into the back of the truck. Hopping in the back beside them, I began to fold the papers for delivery.

Bruce and I soon worked out a system. I'd rap on the roof of the cab when we came to a customer's house, take a paper and run up the many, many stairs to deliver it at the front door. Our village, which was terraced, was built on the narrow strip of land that lay between the mountains and the ocean. In the winter, the locals got their paper through the mail, but the summer people wanted the latest paper, not one three days old. And they wanted it right on their doorstep, even if that doorstep was two flights of stairs up from the bottom of their property.

"Too bad you can't drive," Bruce said partway through the route. "We could change jobs halfway through."

"I can drive. My brother, Sam, taught me."

"Next time."

"You're all dressed up," said Mom. "Are you going to the dance again?" I was wearing my new red, short-sleeved sweater and white cotton skirt patterned with crimson roses.

"Yes, and Bruce Hanson is giving me a ride home . . . It's not like it's a date or anything," I hurried to explain as I saw a look of disapproval begin to cloud her eyes. "It's his sister Anna. She wants him to go to the dance. She's got a date, and she wants to spend all her time with him. She told me that Bruce won't dance with the summer girls there because he doesn't know them, and he doesn't want to get to know them."

"Bruce is that way. Always a bit standoffish. It's been worse since the woman he was engaged to in Halifax dumped him. She broke off their engagement soon after his ship was torpedoed." Mom grimaced. "Burns all over," she said, running her hands down the front of her body to indicate the extent. Then she clapped her hands to both ears. "Even inside his ears. He wasn't expected to live, let alone live any kind of normal life. Mrs. Hanson was beside herself. The whole thing was just too bad. Some don't blame the young woman for not wanting to marry him — the shape he was in — but he took it hard. Very hard. I'm surprised he's dancing again. Of course, when his sister Anna makes up her mind about anything, it gets done. So if Anna has decided that Bruce is going to get back to some sort of social life, then it's going to happen."

"I didn't know all this."

"We don't tell you children everything . . . Don't stay out too late. You're working in the morning."

The dance floor was almost full when Bruce and I arrived. Amy and Glen were dancing in the corner of the room, heads bent towards each other like two birds. I spotted Anna and her date, a tall man in a soldier's uniform. He was holding her tightly, and she had a dreamy smile on her face.

Once we started to dance, I forgot all about everyone except Bruce. To be moving with the music in the soft summer night, his hand firm on my back, was my idea of heaven. They were playing Benny Goodman's "Taking a Chance on Love." Yes, I thought, you take a chance when you fall in love.

The set finished about twenty minutes later, and Bruce and I stood there waiting for the next one to begin. Out of the corner of my eye, I saw Amy leave Glen and head straight for us.

"Meg, I'd like to be introduced to your partner," Amy said. "And you can dance with Glen." Amy stepped in closer to Bruce and smiled up at him.

Bruce stepped back. The music started. Without even a glance of acknowledgement to Amy, Bruce took my hand, and we were out on the floor dancing before I had a chance to really register what had happened.

I watched Amy turn and head back in Glen's direction. Her spine was rigid. She held her shoulders so high they almost reached her ears.

She was too late for Glen. He was already up and dancing with a summer girl, an older girl about eighteen. Her family came up to the Landing every summer in their yacht. I won't have to worry about Amy again tonight, I thought. She'll be too intent on getting Glen back.

Just then, Robert Pryce came in the door with his wife and Glen's mother and stepfather. They all began to dance. Dr. Barras, a big man, was surprising graceful.

Without warning, the loud sounds of a man's shouting came up the path and in the open doorway. Everyone looked over that way to see Sylvia Ballard's husband stumble inside. He looked wildly around, his eyes finally settling on Robert Pryce.

Mr. Ballard made a beeline for Robert.

The next thing I knew, Bruce was pulling me through the door and outside. He took my hand and folded it around a key. "Go down to the truck, lock the doors and stay there. Ballard needs my help right now before he does something stupid. I'll be with you as soon as I can."

Inside the truck, I could hear the music from the tennis

court. It seemed a long time before Bruce came, but it probably wasn't more than ten minutes. He had Mr. Ballard with
him.

Mr. Ballard was weaving all over the path and into the
bushes. Bruce struggled to hold him upright. I saw Mr. Ballard stumble. He almost took Bruce down with him.

I unlocked the doors, got out and helped Bruce guide Mr.
Ballard into the passenger seat. Then I climbed in beside him.
Bruce staggered to the driver's door and fell into the seat. He
had trouble turning on the ignition. In the light from the
dashboard, I could see that he had a cut over his right eye and
a swelling in the same cheek, extending up to the ear. He was
pale, and his face held an unhealthy sheen of perspiration.

"I'm driving, Bruce," I said.

I got out of the passenger side and slid in beside Bruce.

He didn't argue, but moved over and let me in behind the
wheel. Easing the truck down to the main road, finally I had
it headed in the direction of the Ballards'. Once there, in spite
of grinding the gears a few times, I leaned on the horn until
Mrs. Ballard came to the front door.

"Hurry," I called to her from the open truck window.
"Come get your husband."

She stared at me from the lighted doorway.

"Hurry!" I shouted. Finally she walked over slowly. I helped
her get her husband inside their house.

I didn't say anything to Bruce all the way back to the Hansons'. For one thing, I needed to concentrate on driving. For

another, his breathing had become rapid and shallow. Parking in front of the Hansons' and turning the engine off, I said, "Bruce, I'm going in to get your mother. Stay here."

I went into the Hansons' and heard Mrs. Hanson's voice coming from upstairs. She was talking very loudly, and her voice was not her usual calm and placid one. This was her strictly no-nonsense tone, the kind she used with the Co-op grocery store in Gibson's if they were late with their delivery.

"I must ask you both to calm down," she said. "I cannot have this disturbance. I have other guests, and they must be considered."

Glen's mother answered in a conciliatory way, "You must excuse my husband, Mrs. Hanson. He's had a very trying evening. Family business, you know. You understand how that can be. We will be leaving tomorrow on the noon boat . . . No, of course we don't expect a refund. Again, my apologies."

I waited until Mrs. Hanson came downstairs, her footsteps a heavy thud on the steps. Her face was red, and she was breathing hard. "Really," she muttered, slamming her way into the kitchen.

"Bruce's outside in the truck," I said quickly. "I'll need help bringing him inside. He's been staggering. I think he's in pain, too."

She looked at me, worry sharp in her eyes. "What happened?"

"I don't know, except I think he was trying to stop a fight between Mr. Ballard and Robert Pryce."

"That's like Bruce, all right . . . Maybe one of them accidentally hit Bruce's bad ear, the ear that was burned. Once we get him in bed, I'll phone Dr. Casey. Pray God that he's not out delivering a baby somewhere up the peninsula."

Bruce staggered even more once we got him into the bright kitchen. The hall to his bedroom was dimly lit, as was his room, and he seemed to walk better with less light. I knew where his bed was located — I'd made it often enough — and we soon had him there and lying down. Mrs. Hanson left to phone the doctor.

It was hard to see clearly without the light on, but the grimace of pain was easing from Bruce's face, and he seemed more like himself. As I was leaving him to join Mrs. Hanson in the kitchen, he said quietly, "You're a sweetheart, Meg."

Mrs. Hanson was still talking on the phone. "Just a minute, Dr. Casey, and I'll check . . . No, no vomiting . . . No, not dizzy . . . Some staggering. Pain, yes . . . His right ear . . . Yes, the one that was burned in the explosion . . . Yes, I'll bring him up to you immediately if there are any more problems . . . All right, tomorrow morning at ten. Thank you, Dr. Casey."

By the time I got home, it was late. "I'm not happy about this, Meg," Mom said.

But when I told her what had happened, she softened. "You did well," she said. "As for Mrs. Ballard . . . Well, what we do affects other people, and she's too old to have been acting up the way she has."

Chapter Nine

✻

ON MY WAY TO WORK the next morning, I called in on Amy to ask her about the fight between Robert Pryce and Mr. Ballard the night before. Mrs. Miller met me at the door, still in her pale blue baby-doll nightgown.

"Amy's gone out in the boat with the Pryce boy," Mrs. Miller said. "No, I'm sorry, I don't have any idea when she'll be back."

There was no sign of Bruce when I went into work. Anna looked up from rolling out a pie crust and smiled at me. She eased the pie crust carefully into the waiting pie plate and began to trim it, humming as she did so.

"Your date turned out okay?" I said.

"Better than okay."

Upstairs, I found three suitcases outside the door of Dr. Barras' room. The door was slightly ajar, and the sounds of a quarrel carried out into the hallway. Although Dr. and Mrs. Barras were trying to whisper, the voices seemed to carry even further than if spoken normally. It was all the sibilants, I decided. They sounded like snakes hissing.

The doctor's voice was angry. "No, I do take it seriously. Seriously, I say. Rob Pryce being attacked by an outraged husband at the dance last night. His brother, your son, Glen . . . acting like a randy teenager. The girl hanging onto him . . . no better. I don't want your son bringing this kind of chaos into our household. Think of our children."

Glen's mother's voice was soothing. "Don't upset yourself, Harold. Think of your blood pressure. Leave it to me. I'll take care of everything."

That afternoon when the *Lady Cecilia* called in on her return trip to Vancouver, I made sure I was sweeping the porch outside. From there, I could see the gangplank. Glen was there with his mother. But instead of following her up onto the ship, as I'd expected, he bent his head and kissed her on the cheek, as if in goodbye.

I didn't see Bruce until later that day. He looked much better and wanted something to eat. I cut a slice of homemade bread, toasted it and slathered on the butter. The coffee was newly brewed, and I poured him a cup, adding extra cream and sugar. He looked tired, and the bruise in front of his right ear was an angry purple. But at least he was no longer staggering.

"Thanks for last night," he said quietly. "You came through like the trooper I know you to be."

From then on, every time we met he'd smile briefly, or give me a thumbs-up.

"I'm worried about Bruce," Mrs. Hanson said to Anna a few days later as she kneaded the bread dough. "I don't think he should be out fishing. The glare off the water could make him dizzy, and he's out there all alone. Dr. Casey did tell me that with Bruce's ear injury, bright light could bring on a spell of dizziness. But he needs to be doing something. He's getting impatient waiting for this last skin graft."

"Did the doctor say it's okay for him to go dancing?" Anna said.

"I asked, and he said, 'Yes, encourage him to do it.' You remember what the burn doctor said when Bruce was first in the hospital? That burn victims need to be encouraged to get back with people, back to being social? 'So many of them,' he said, 'think that they are too disfigured for people to want to be with them.'"

Bruce disfigured? That small patch on his chest? Where else? Was that why he sometimes seemed blunt, even ungracious?

"How is Alfred Kallio?" asked Mrs. Hanson, giving the

dough a good *thump* to knock out the air bubbles. "Did you have a nice time last night? I heard you come in. It was very late."

"He's asked me to marry him," said Anna.

"That was fast."

"He says that they're being shipped overseas after they finish basic training."

Mrs. Hanson sighed. "Will there ever be an end to this war? There's not a family on this peninsula who hasn't someone in the services. Well, it's not as if you haven't known Alfred for a long time. And he's from good stock. I knew his mother's people."

"We thought we'd get married at the end of August. We'll take a weekend for a honeymoon before he has to go back to base. And things will be slowing down here at the guest house. It seems like a good time."

"I don't know, Anna. To get ready for a big wedding in that short a time . . ."

"No big wedding, Mama. A trip to City Hall and an overnight stay at the Hotel Georgia, that's all we've planned."

"Bruce, do you think I could go out fishing with you?" I asked the next time we were alone in the kitchen drinking coffee. "I'd like to learn."

"Learn to fish?" he said, suspicion in his rising voice. "There's not much to it."

"I'd like to learn how to handle an inboard, too. I thought

you were going to be a big brother to me, since mine's away in the Air Force. He'd teach me if I asked him."

"Meg, you're not fooling me. You think I'll get dizzy out in the boat with the sunlight glaring off the water . . . My mother has put you up to this."

"No, she hasn't. Why are you so miserable all the time? Can't you believe that I like to learn things? Or even that I like being with you?"

He put his coffee cup down with a rattle.

I'd gone too far. "As a friend," I hurried to add.

"Friend?"

"Yes, friend. What's the matter with that? As a friend, I want to be with you if you need my help, like, say you do get dizzy . . ."

For a moment, I thought he was going to push his chair back and leave, but then his eyes lost their sharpness and even softened. "It will mean you'll have to set your alarm. I like to be out on the water when the tide changes. I'm talking five o'clock tomorrow morning. If you're not at the float on time, I'm leaving anyway." I could hear the naval officer in the way he spoke.

I couldn't remember ever getting up that early before. The sky was beginning to lighten in the east as I left home quietly and made my way to the wharf. Bruce was already down at the float with the fishing gear, water and an extra can of gas.

The ocean was absolutely flat, and we made our way out to

Salmon Rock in good time. We used live herring for bait, and the salmon hit almost immediately. Bruce had me tend one line while he took care of the other. In an hour and a half, we had caught seven good-sized coho.

The water had begun to pick up a chop, and the sun bounced off the waves, reflecting like a hundred mirrors. I was relieved when Bruce put on sunglasses and pulled the peak of his cap down lower.

I had watched how he handled the boat and thought I knew a few basics, though I wasn't sure about starting the engine if I had to. I saw that Bruce had turned the flywheel over by hand, and I thought I could do that. The engine had its own sound. *Two bits two bits two bits*, it putted across the water. Bruce said it was an Easthope. "Single cylinder, water-cooled. I like the Easthope better than a Briggs and Stratton."

"So do I," I said.

"Meg, you're full of it," he said, but he grinned.

We got back to the Landing without any trouble. After we had tied up at the float, Bruce began to clean the salmon. He picked one up, slit the belly open with one swift cut of his knife and dropped the guts into the ocean beside us.

"Want to try?" he asked, leaning back on his heels.

"Sure." He handed me the knife. I found that it wasn't as easy as it looked. I finished one salmon and handed the knife back. "I'll do two next time," I said.

Mrs. Hanson smiled with pleasure at the sight of our catch. "Our new guests will rave about my sour cream and onion salmon," she said. "Come, sit down, the two of you. For you, I'll make pancakes, bacon and eggs. The coffee's freshly made." She filled two cups and placed them before us.

"Do you like fishing that much, Meg, that you'd get up so early for it?" she asked as she busied herself at the stove.

"I like being out on the water," I said. "Fishing's just an excuse to be out there. I don't even like the taste of salmon that much."

"Wait until you've eaten my special baked salmon. A Norwegian neighbour gave me the recipe years ago. I'll save some for you from dinner tonight."

I felt sleepy after the huge breakfast, and I didn't know how I was going to stay awake for work in an hour. Mrs. Hanson caught me nodding.

"You can catch a few winks in one of the bedrooms upstairs in the attic," she said. "I keep a couple of rooms ready there in case of an emergency. I see you brought a change of clothing. But mind you take off your shoes. My mother made those quilts. I'll wake you in time for work."

The room was small but cozy. On the bedside table, a family album lay open to two pictures of Bruce. In one, he was about three and held a cat. He was holding it carefully, its head supported, cradling it in his arms. In the other, he looked about seven and held a baby, his cousin Rita, according to the writing on the back. His blond head, perfectly shaped, was bent over the baby in a caring way. This was the Bruce I sensed was there under his often abrupt manner.

My days were full, yet I missed Amy. She was always with Glen. Every few days I would stop by to see her.

One early afternoon, I knocked and knocked at her front door and had finally given up and turned away when the door opened. Amy stood there, swaying. She looked dazed. Sleepy-eyed. Face slack.

Beyond the open door, I saw Glen lying on the couch with the same stunned look on his face. I must have interrupted their lovemaking, I thought. The air was thick with their sexual tension. I fled, mumbling something about coming back another time.

The scene stayed with me for days. It seemed that everywhere I looked, I saw people in love, falling in love, making love. It made me curious, excited, with strong, unexpected yearnings. But I also felt uneasy, not really ready to know any more about this new world.

These feelings grew even stronger when my brother, Sam, came home on a one-week leave from the Air Force with his girlfriend Olive, a newly graduated nurse. "I want to wait until after the war before we get married," she told my mother.

"Very sensible," Mom commented.

"Meg must come and visit my family some time," Olive said. "I have two sisters, and they would love her. She would fit right in. They are fifteen and eighteen."

"It would be good for Meg to be with girls," Mom said.

"There's only one girl here in the Landing, and she's a — well, should I say a bit too mature for her age?"

Olive helped dry while I washed the dishes. "I think yellow would be a good colour on you," she said. "Especially with your dark hair and eyes. Are they hazel or brown? My eighteen-year-old sister loves makeup, and I think she'll want to show you all she knows. Promise that you'll come and stay with us for a weekend before you start school in September."

Sam came outside to talk to me one morning when I was hanging up the weekly wash on the clothesline. "Mother says you're working at Mrs. Hanson's Guest House," he said. "How are they treating you?"

"Fine." I reached for a pillowcase. "Couldn't be nicer."

"Bruce, too?"

"Yes. He's fine, too. Why do you ask?" I reeled out the clothesline.

"I went to high school with him. I didn't much like him. He thought he was better than anyone else."

"Sometimes he acts that way," I said.

"He went off to university. Did well. There was no putting up with him after that."

"He lost a lot of his shipmates when his ship was torpedoed. And you know that he got badly burned. He told me that it changed him a lot," I said.

"It would, yes . . . I used to think that his mother and sister made too much of him. So did the teachers."

"Well, he's okay with me, Sam. And I'm making good money and have a chance for more work off-season."

"I'm just warning you not to go getting a crush on Bruce. He's kind of old for you, anyway."

I glared at him. "Oh, mind your own damn business! Stop acting like a big brother!"

But maybe I *was* getting a crush on Bruce Hanson. I found I was thinking about him all the time. From the moment I woke up until it came time to lay my head on the pillow at night, he was there in my mind.

When we were out fishing and he was baiting a hook, I saw how the sun glistened in the hairs on his arms, making them golden. I noticed how his shirt stretched across his shoulders when he pulled up a salmon. Often he hadn't shaved before we went out on the boat, and I wondered if the stubble would scratch against my cheek.

That he didn't know what I was thinking, I was sure. His manner towards me remained much the same. He was often brusque, sometimes silent, occasionally warm, always protective.

"I want to talk to you about something that's been on my mind," he said one morning, just before we headed the boat back to the Landing. Our catch lay on the floorboards between us, their scales shining like miniature rainbows in the sun. "It's about Amy."

"Oh, yes. My friend, Amy."

"She's not really a good friend for you, Meg. I think she uses you. She says 'come,' and you do. She says 'go,' and you do that, too."

"What makes you say that?"

"I notice things," he said. "Once that Pryce boy goes into Vancouver to work, she'll want you dancing attendance on her again. Not that he's any prize either. What he needs is a good stint in the services to make a man out of him."

"I guess."

"Meg, what you should be doing is applying to different universities for their scholarships. There must be ones available for girls. UBC isn't the only university. Write to McGill, Queen's . . ."

"I've got all year to do that," I said. Sam, now Bruce, bossing me around . . .

"But if there is a scholarship for someone making the highest marks in English, or history, you could be doing extra reading and studying right now. There are government correspondence courses you could take that would broaden your knowledge."

"Why are you so ambitious for me, Bruce?"

"Because you're intelligent, hard-working, and I think you could make your mark on the world with the right education . . ."

"Bruce, I think your line's moving."

He turned quickly to check it. "No, it isn't."

He looked back at me. "I care about you, Meg."

"You care about me?"

"Well, yes, I care about what happens to you . . . I'm ambitious for you. I'm ambitious for me, too. One more skin graft to go — the most important one — and when that's done and finished with, I'm going after a degree in law. I intend to stay with the Navy and make it my career."

But I was still thinking about, "I care about you, Meg."

At the end of July, Amy told me that Glen was leaving the Landing to live with his mother, stepfather and their children in Vancouver. "He had his doubts," she said, "but his mother begged him. He says he'll visit me on his day off from caddying at the University Golf Course."

When Glen came, he and Amy didn't have much time to visit. The Union Steamship came into the Landing at noon, continued on up the Sound to Seaside Park, and returned to the Landing three hours later to pick up passengers bound for Vancouver.

For those three hours, no one saw much of Glen and Amy. They pretty much had the Miller house to themselves. Mrs. Miller was spending most of her time with new friends she'd made at Sechelt. The friends had a car and would call for her.

August brought bad news. Robert Pryce's wife was being sent to the TB Sanitarium at Tranquille. She'd had TB when she was younger, and recent X-rays showed a large shadow on her left lung. She would need to be at the "San" for at least a year.

All of this was told to me by Amy, who was waiting for me

almost every day when I got off work at 5:00. Bruce still disapproved of her and said so. "Now that she doesn't have that young boy around, she wants your company," he said.

"What does it matter to you?" I said. He had been particularly irritable all week, and I wondered if it was something I'd done, or said.

"Just warning you, that's all. I don't like to see you being used. Your nature's too trusting."

I kept silent.

"Okay, sorry. Sorry about being so cranky, too. It's not your fault that I can't wait to get this surgery over and done with. I want to get on with my life . . . Go ahead, Meg. Amy's waiting for you right now. Just don't say I didn't warn you."

One afternoon, when Amy called for me after work, she said, "Just thought I'd walk home with you." Along the way, she kept sighing and pulling at her hair. A couple of times she started to say something, but broke off abruptly. All the while, her face grew more and more anxious.

Finally I stopped in the middle of the road and faced her. With autumn coming on, the leaves in the forest behind Amy had started to change colour. Some were as yellow as the sweater she wore. Her eyes were the same shade of blue as the mountains in the background. She had never looked so beautiful — except for the worry lines in her forehead.

"What's the matter, Amy? Tell me."

"Oh, Meg, I think I'm pregnant."

Chapter Ten

❧

"DOES GLEN KNOW?" I asked.

"Not yet. I'm waiting another week before I go to see Dr. Casey. But my period's already three weeks late, and my breasts are starting to tingle."

"Oh, Amy! What are you going to do?"

"We could get married."

"But Glen is going to UBC."

"He could still do that. I'll stay here and finish grade twelve, and he can come up once a week, the way he does now."

She counted off on nine fingers. "April. The baby would be due in April. Glen would be finished at UBC by then. We'll be fine."

She made it sound so simple.

"The kids at school will turn their back on me, though. Meg, you have to promise you'll stick by me and be my friend."

"Of course I will, Amy," I said. "You know that." Her face lost some of its tight look.

The following days dragged. I saw Amy every day, and every day she shook her head. "No period, yet," she said.

At the end of the week, she decided it was time to see the doctor. "I'll go after school," she said. "I'm nervous, and I want you to come with me. Meg, could you lend me five dollars for the doctor's visit? I don't want to ask my mother. She would want to know why. I'll pay you back as soon as I can."

Outside the doctor's office, Amy asked me to wait. I heard the *Lady Alexandra* whistle as she left Keats Island. I watched her slowly swing her bow towards Gibson's Landing. Twenty minutes later, Amy came out with the news.

"I'm six weeks pregnant," she said. "Dr. Casey is worried because of my age, and I have to see him every month. Now all I have to do is tell Glen. I can't wait until he comes up — I'm going to phone him right now." She sighed. "I'm not sure how he's going to take it, but . . ."

Once we were back at the Landing, we went to the village store, and Amy placed the phone call. She asked for Glen, listened a few minutes, said goodbye and hung up. "His mother says he's at work," she said, turning to me. "She'll have him phone his brother Robert's house at seven tonight. I'm to be there to receive the call. Come with me. Okay, Meg?"

We were at the Pryce house by 6:30. Robert answered the door, and when Amy explained that Glen would be phoning, Robert led us into the living room.

This was my first time inside the Pryce home. Even though Mrs. Pryce was away in the sanitarium, the room looked tidy and well-cared-for. It was an attractive room with polished dark oak floors, a bright, oval rug in the middle of the living room, a fireplace of huge stones and cedar panelling on the walls. I saw oil paintings and small sculptures. A bookcase lined one wall.

Amy sank into the nearest large leather armchair. I perched nervously on an unstable rosewood chair upholstered with petit point. I was almost afraid to breathe because Mrs. Pryce's TB germs probably still lingered in the air. The phone sat mute and black on a teak end table.

I wondered how Amy would be able to talk privately to Glen with Robert settled in another leather chair nearby. The grandfather clock in the corner started to chime out the hours. "Mr. Pryce," I said, "may I have a drink of water, please?"

"The kitchen is at the back of the house," he said. He settled himself more firmly in his armchair. His eyes didn't leave Amy.

"Would you mind showing me, please? I really hate to bother you, Mr. Pryce. But it's your house and all, and I don't want to invade your privacy."

He looked at me as if I were a complete idiot. Muttering something under his breath, he dragged himself up from the chair and turned towards the rear of the house.

The phone rang. Robert Pryce froze where he was. He stood listening.

"Oh, Glen, I'm so glad you phoned," Amy said. "Well, yes. I'm . . . well . . ." She lowered her voice to a whisper, but it was still audible. "I'm pregnant . . . No, I'm sure, I've been to the doctor . . . Yes . . . April . . . When are you coming up? We have to talk."

Mr. Pryce turned to me, his face blank. "I think you can find the kitchen yourself," he said, returning to his armchair.

"Yes. Thanks," I said and left a wide space between us as I passed him.

Tuesday, Sept 5, 1944

Dear Journal,

Glen came up last Thursday to see Amy. She seems sublimely confident that everything will work out. I think I'm more worried and upset about her being pregnant than she is. I asked her how she could be so calm, and she said, "I have Rob's support. He told me so. Said he'd be glad to see me in the family, that they all know I'm not a 'run-around' like my mother."

Personally, I think that's an awful thing for Robert Pryce to say. I like Mrs. Miller. She's kind of silly, but she's not mean. Besides, who is Robert Pryce to talk about being a "run-around"? I can't help thinking about Mrs. Ballard.

I talked to Olive, my brother's fiancée, about this when I
went in to stay with her and her family over Labour Day
weekend. She's a nurse and very nice. So are her whole
family. Her sisters plan to be nurses, and I've decided
that's what I want to do, too, be a nurse. Olive is
understanding and kind. I'd like to be just like her.

The first day of school, my brother, Dan, and I found a new boy waiting at our bus stop. He wasn't bad looking: medium height, freckles, sandy hair, blue-green eyes. He said his name was Jack Whalan and that he was in grade twelve. "I live on Gambier Island, but I'm boarding here. The school at Port Mellon nearby only goes up to grade eleven."

"Where are you boarding?" I asked.

"Mrs. Thompson's. Her son Doug is away in the war, and she misses him, so she answered the school board's ad for room and board for a student. I don't have his room, though. She keeps it like a shrine. Pictures of him all over, sport trophies. I think she's —"

"You're lucky to be boarding there," I interrupted. "She's a very nice person."

He turned away and said to Dan, "I saw a few grouse along the road the other day. Do you ever go shooting?"

They talked about .22s until the bus came. As soon as we got on the bus, I headed back to where Amy was sitting. She looked white, almost as if she were going to faint.

"I feel sick," she said. "But I don't think I have anything more to throw up."

"Here." I passed her a small package of soda crackers from my lunch kit. "Olive, Sam's girlfriend, is a nurse, and she says they'll help. Just eat a couple at a time . . . Why don't we move to the front of the bus? Maybe if you sit behind the driver and look straight ahead, you won't feel so sick."

We made it to school without Amy throwing up and walked down the long field to the high school. No amount of white paint could disguise that it had once been a shack in a logging camp. It still sat on its logging skids.

Mr. Freeman, the principal of both the elementary and high school and who also taught grades 9 to 12, smiled at us as we stepped into the room. Amy left me to talk to her friend, Louise.

"Ah, you must be Jack," Mr. Freeman said as the new boy came in the door. "You can take the second seat from the front in the grade twelve row. Meg, show Jack where that is."

The grade twelve row was by the windows. I slipped into the seat at the front. Jack sat behind me and opened the top of his desk. I felt him tap on my shoulder, and I looked around.

"I'm taking a correspondence course in chemistry," he said. "Mr. Freeman is arranging it. He wants me to have a partner for the lab. Do you want to be my partner?"

"Well, I took Latin by correspondence last year," I said. I was silent as I thought of my correspondence instructor who had written on one of the papers, "You are doing very well in this course. What are you planning to do with your knowledge of Latin?"

"I'd like to be a brain surgeon," I had written back on my

next paper. What an impossible dream. I didn't even know any women doctors. Nursing would be the closest I could ever get.

Jack's words broke into my thoughts. "Hey, you still with me?"

"Yes. I was thinking about something. I'm thinking of going into nurses' training when I finish this year. Chemistry would help, wouldn't it?"

He nodded. "Mr. Freeman says he is going to make the utility room into a lab."

I could see the utility room from where I sat. It was a small, crowded, dingy room with a single window streaked with dirt. "It wouldn't matter if we blew that place up," I said. "I saw a rat in there, once."

"Does that mean yes?"

"I guess so." Bruce would approve. I'd ask Mr. Freeman, at the same time, about universities that might offer scholarships to girls.

At recess, I looked for Amy but couldn't see her. I walked up alone to the girls' washroom in the elementary school. Everyone stopped talking as soon as I went in. They stared at me.

"So, Meg, your friend's got herself pregnant," a grade twelve girl called out. "I bet you hope it's not catching."

I tried to ignore the staring faces and got out of there as soon as I could. An excited buzz of voices followed me out the door.

I debated whether to tell Amy or not. Though I looked for

her, I didn't see her at lunchtime, or at afternoon recess either. After the last class, I found her waiting at the school bus stop.

"Where have you been all day?" I said.

"Lying down in the nurse's room."

I told her what had happened at morning recess.

"That must have been Louise who spread the news," Amy said. "I told her this morning, but she promised she wouldn't tell anyone. I guess you can't trust anyone, even your best friend."

"I didn't say anything to anyone!"

"Not you," Amy said. "I meant Louise."

"*Oh.*"

As the weeks passed, I noticed a subtle change in the attitude of the other girls. I wasn't the best softball player, but in the past when teams had been chosen, at least my name had been called about midway through. Now I was the last one picked. If I fumbled a ball, or made it late to a base, the jeers were louder than for anyone else.

Taunting began. "Friends with Amy! Everyone knows she sleeps around. Hey, Magpie, do you have round heels, too? Are you going to get pregnant next? Who's the poor jerk you've picked to be the father?"

I think that if Amy had been at school more often instead of staying at home, less might have been said to me. But she was away from school a lot. For the past two weeks, she'd been on bed rest, Dr. Casey's orders.

"He says my blood pressure is too high, and my legs are

swollen. I'm not allowed to have salt, and I have to take a urine sample to him every week."

Mr. Freeman gave me homework to take to Amy, and I delivered it to her every afternoon. Even though she had headaches, she did the work he'd assigned. Not only that, she had started sewing baby clothes by hand. I could hardly believe that she was patient enough to make the tiny stitches.

The correspondence course in chemistry turned out to be much harder than I'd thought. So much to memorize! It helped to have Jack as my partner — he seemed to know everything. The makeshift lab in the utility room was too small, and we kept bumping into each other. Each time we did, I found I reacted physically to him. The hardness of his body caused strange stirrings in the pit of my stomach. This must be what Amy feels with Glen, I thought. Though I didn't especially like Jack, every time I looked at him, excitement flushed through my body. I'd felt this before with Glen and Bruce.

One late fall day when the maple tree outside our lab window had dropped the last of its golden leaves, Jack said, "Would you like to go to the Halloween dance with me? I've asked around about you. I hear good things. My landlady Mrs. Thompson says you were kind to her son Doug and wrote to him when he joined the Army. The kids here think you're smart and a hard worker. But," and his voice harshened, "it's too bad you're friends with that girl."

"That girl?"

"The one who's in the family way."

"Are you talking about Amy?"

"It makes you look bad. You know, to choose her for a friend."

"About the dance. Thanks for asking, but no. The answer is no."

His pupils grew big with surprise. "Because of what I said about your friend?"

"Yes."

"I hope you'll think about it. It would be fun."

I looked at the clock on the classroom wall. "I've got to go. I'll leave you to wash out the test tubes."

"But you always wash the test tubes!"

"From now on, we're taking turns."

Chapter Eleven

❋

AFTER I'D PICKED UP the mail later that afternoon, I saw Bruce burning leaves at the beach in front of the guest house. The air was sweet with their incense. An October sky of brilliant blue vaulted over the calm ocean. Out on the water, an outboard thrummed its way towards the open Gap.

Bruce looked up from the pile of leaves he was forking into the flames. We'd seen each other every Saturday when I'd gone to help Mrs. Hanson, and I'd already told him about taking chemistry. "Great!" he'd said. This time, I wanted to talk to him about Jack and what he'd said about Amy.

"I know you say I need to be careful not to let Amy, or anyone, use me." I took a long stick and turned a pile of smoldering leaves until it flared again. "I don't think what Jack says is the same thing."

"Let's talk a minute," Bruce said, and we left the fire and sat on a nearby log. I brushed some ashes from his grey sweater. I noticed it was beginning to unravel at both cuffs.

"Of course, it's different," he said. "We're talking about loyalty. Loyalty is good. Your sense of loyalty is one of the things I like about you."

"Oh . . . What else do you like?"

He laughed. "Oh, that you found the cameo that belonged to one of the guests and gave it back to her. You could have kept it for yourself . . . Back to loyalty. It's not that common, I've found."

Was he thinking of his fiancée, who had called off the engagement after he'd been burned?

"I know how much you like to dance, Meg, and I'll bet this boy will ask you again. Say 'yes.' Go. Have a good time. It's a way of getting to know boys, men, so that later, when you decide to get married, you'll know what kind of man you want."

"I'll think about it."

"So you do want to get married?"

"Oh, sometime, I guess."

"And have children?"

"I'm in no hurry," I said.

"I'd ask you to go to the Halloween dance with me — I want to dance with you again — but I never know when I'm going to get a phone call from the hospital to go in for my last skin graft. It's supposed to be soon."

I liked the way he was looking at me, as if I gave him plea-sure. Now the tingling sensations were back in my body again. So it wasn't just being bumped into by Jack in the small lab. I was growing up, and for the first time I felt more excited than scared.

Bruce tucked my hand into his. My heart stopped.

"This may not be the best time to talk to you about this . . . You're special to me. I want the very best for you. For you to finish your education, to go into nurses' training, if that's what you decide to do. Maybe when you're older, twenty-one or so, you might think it's time to get married. In the mean-time, I'll get my law degree, and maybe my skin graft will be successful . . . Well, enough of that for now. Lots of maybes, I know. But keep it in mind, because I . . ." He stopped.

"You what?" I asked.

"I can be loyal, too."

I sat stunned. Unbelieving. I must have misunderstood him. He couldn't possibly have said what I thought he'd said.

We didn't talk about it anymore. The rest of the afternoon was spent burning leaves. A quiet hum had started inside of me. I knew I must have misunderstood him. It was an im-possible dream. Yet I kept thinking about it anyway.

It was enough for now that his eyes said he was happy to be with me. The fire turned to red embers, the air cooled as the sun went down, but the humming inside went on and on.

Jack did ask me to the dance again, and, thinking about what Bruce had said, I decided to go.

At work at the Hanson's on Saturday, the first thing I did was look around for Bruce to tell him.

"He's gone," said Mrs. Hanson. "The hospital phoned two days ago, and he went in on the next boat. He left you a note, though." She took an envelope from behind the kitchen clock and handed it to me.

"For today, I want you to work on the bedrooms in the attic. Now that the mill at Port Mellon is running again, I've had a lot of mill workers looking for room and board. You'll need to take a mop to the walls. I don't know where all the dust comes from. And after that, start on the floors. Wash and wax."

As soon as I was alone, I opened the envelope and read Bruce's note:

Dear Meg,

Sorry I didn't get to see you before I left, but there wasn't time. The doctors tell me it's going to be a long haul, and visitors might be restricted at first because of the risk of infection. I'd like it if you wrote to me. Tell me how you are doing. You know I'm always interested.

Bruce

The community hall was decorated with orange and black crepe-paper streamers, cut-outs of skeletons, witches and pumpkins. I saw Mr. and Mrs. Ballard. He was dressed as a pirate; she wore a gypsy skirt, blouse and dangling earrings. When I told Mom I had to say no when Mrs. Ballard had asked me to babysit, she had said, "I know you want to go to the dance, Meg. Tell Mrs. Ballard I'll fill in for you. I'm just so glad things are settling down for those two that I don't mind helping out."

Jack led me out onto the dance floor that was slippery with talcum powder. His dancing was forceful and strong. A couple of times, he stepped on my right foot. Both times he said, "You have to let me lead." As if it were my fault. I knew from both Glen and Bruce that I was a good dancer, but I decided to let it go. I found it hard to like Jack, in spite of admiring him for his brains. I was still surprised at the strong physical attraction I felt every time I was near him.

He was attentive. At intermission, he seated me on one of the benches that lined the hall and said, "I'll be back in a minute. Don't go away."

He returned, grinning all the way across the dance floor, carrying an ice cream cone. He seemed so pleased that I couldn't help thinking that I was too critical of him. My heart softened.

We walked home together after the dance. When we got to the top of the path leading down to my house, he bent his head to kiss me. I stepped back.

"Aww, Meg," he said. "Come on."

"Goodnight, Jack," I said. The wind sighed in the cedar trees. I wished it were Bruce who had wanted to kiss me.

Amy was back at school, a slight bump puffing out the loose tops she wore. Ever since I'd gone to the dance with Jack, the kids had stopped bugging me about being friends with Amy. She and I spent recesses and lunches together and sat beside each other on the bus.

Jack didn't say anything more about my friendship with Amy. We were too busy trying to outdo each other at school. He would get an A. I'd study even harder to keep up with him. Mr. Freeman beamed.

I knew that Jack would always be better at chemistry than I was, but I tried to learn from him. "I'm going to university and then on to grad school in the States," he told me. "I'm going to do basic research."

"You'll be good at it," I said and meant it. I knew he would have to do it on scholarships alone, with no help from his family.

He had told me about his family one afternoon after we got off the school bus. He said that his own parents were divorced, that his father was a navigator in the Air Force and that he had a stepfather. "He's jealous of me and my mother. He wants her all to himself. I hate him. He's logging on Gambier Island where we live, making up booms. One day I was down at the beach, and I happened to look up at the top of the cliff. I saw him about to roll a huge log down on me. I jumped out of the way and yelled back, 'If you ever try that again, I'll kill you.'"

I looked at him quickly. He must be making this up, I thought. But his jaw was rigid, and I believed him. I could see Jack saying and doing exactly that.

I'd seen the same look on his face one evening when we'd

gone to the Friday night movie at the community hall at Gibson's. We were supposed to meet there at 8:00, and when he didn't turn up, I found a seat on my own. About twenty minutes later, he came in, short of breath and with his fists clenched at his sides. He told me that three or four of the high school boys had ganged up on him. "You think you're so smart," they'd said. Cliff Olson, the biggest one, had started hammering him.

"I knocked him down with my first punch," Jack said. "He didn't know I was light-weight boxing champ at Port Mellon this summer."

I craned my neck around to see if Cliff was there in the hall. He was standing by the back door looking subdued, and I saw him put his hand up and rub his jaw.

I'd never liked Cliff Olson. He farted and burped and made sucking noises whenever he passed a girl. He'd never bothered me, but I think that was because I had brothers.

"He's nothing but a bully," I said now to Jack.

Jack's breathing didn't return to normal for about twenty minutes. I felt the anger in him gradually subside. But he stayed alert.

I didn't know if I liked Jack or not. He had a coldness about him, yet he wrote poetry to me. He seemed to know something about everything, but he didn't know that he sounded conceited when he boasted. I remember what Bruce had said, that I should get to know boys and learn about them. So far, what I'd learned about Jack was that he cared for himself most of all.

Bruce had said he cared about me, what happened to me. Maybe I was making this up. I must be. But I walked around in a daydream anyway, as if it were true.

Bruce hadn't answered any of my letters. I told myself that he was probably not feeling well enough yet, or was in too much pain. Olive had said that burn patients suffered a lot of pain. When I asked Mrs. Hanson how Bruce was, she always said, "We're hopeful."

As the days and weeks passed, I thought that I must have blown up what Bruce had said. Then I would grab my textbooks and concentrate on getting the highest marks I could.

At the beginning of December, Amy's blood pressure climbed dangerously high. Dr. Casey decided to send her to St. Paul's Hospital in Vancouver. She was almost five months pregnant.

"Doc Casey thinks it's pre-eclampsia, and I have to stay on bed rest and have my blood pressure and urine monitored until it's time to deliver. And, oh, Meg, they're going to do a Caesarian. I don't want a scar!"

Amy had more bad news. I was helping her pack a small bag for the hospital, and she was crying when she said, "Glen's father has refused to give his permission for Glen to get married. That means we have to wait four more years for him to be twenty-one, the legal age to marry."

"No wonder Glen hates his father," I said, taking the top she was scrunching into a ball and refolding it to lie flat in the suitcase. "Do you think that Robert could change the father's mind?"

"I've already talked to him about it. He said he'd try. He says that for some reason, their father is harder on Glen than he ever was on the other sons."

Over the Christmas holidays, I went into Vancouver and stayed a few days at Olive's. While there, I caught the streetcar downtown to visit Amy at St. Paul's Hospital. The hallway floors looked like marble and were speckled, like the stones in the creek at the Landing.

Amy was in semi-private on the maternity ward. I could hear the newborns crying from the nursery nearby. A black-robed nun with a starched white wimple glided down the hallway, footless under her black robe. She smiled at me.

I found Glen sitting in the straight-back chair next to Amy's bed.

"I just wanted to say hello, Amy," I said quickly, putting the grapes I'd brought on her bedside table and backing out the door.

Glen followed me out into the hallway. "Thanks for coming," he said. It was the first time he'd spoken to me since that day on Shelter Island in the summer.

"You're welcome." He looked exhausted. "Are you okay?" I asked.

"Well, working every night and going to university at the same time is a killer."

"When do you sleep?"

"From eight to noon. I go to classes in the afternoon then

catch a nap before I go to work at eleven . . . I'm tired all the time."

"Where are you working?"

"At the Hotel Vancouver, as a desk clerk. Pay's not great, but it gives me a chance to study."

"You'd be good at the job. You've had the experience."

"Yeah, the old man trained me well. In fact, the manager knows him, and that was enough for me to get the job."

"How is your mother?"

"She's all right. Dotes on me. That makes it hard on me, though, with her husband and kids. They resent me, I think."

"That's too bad."

"Glen?" called Amy's voice from within the room.

"I'll be right there, Amy."

I told Olive about Bruce being on the burn unit. "I'm not sure how's he's doing. His mother doesn't say much. I'd like to see him, though."

"You could always phone hospital information, give them Bruce's name and ask them to put you through to the nurses' station on his floor. They'd be able to tell you if he is allowed to have visitors . . . The phone is in the kitchen, and the phone book is in the drawer below."

It took awhile to get through the switchboard to the right part of the hospital, but finally, I heard, "Miss Coleman, Heather Pavillion, Medical Floor." I gripped the receiver so close to my ear that both my hand and ear hurt.

"My name is Meg Woods, and I'm a friend of Bruce Hanson. I'm from out of town, and I've written him, but he's never answered . . . Is he dying?"

"Oh, no. No, my dear," the nurse was quick to say. "He had a bad infection, but he's responding well to the new drug we started this week. Penicillin."

"I've heard of it."

"Yes, it's a miracle drug they've been using overseas for our wounded soldiers. We put in a request to Ottawa and had a supply flown in."

"Would you please tell him that I phoned? Meg Woods."

"Meg? Yes, of course, dear. I know it will mean a lot to him. He's talked about you."

"Really? He doesn't usually say much."

"Well, he was pretty sick, there, for a while. Delirious."

Talking about me. Saying my name. My God, maybe he does care, after all.

Now there was no stopping me from going over to the hospital. I stopped at a Chinese grocery store on Broadway and bought a potted poinsettia. The red flowers seemed to shout out the joy that I felt. Bruce said my name.

The Heather Pavillion was one of several buildings of the hospital complex. I got lost looking for it and wound up in a courtyard next to the TB Willow Chest Centre. From there, it took me twenty minutes before I was in the right building and standing before their information desk.

"I'm sorry, visiting hours are over for the afternoon," said the receptionist. "You can leave the flowers here. I'll see that they are delivered to Mr. Hanson. Come back at seven."

"I won't be here then. I'm from out of town, and I'm catching the boat back this evening. Could I just pop up and leave them myself?" I asked. "I'll just say hello."

"Up the stairs, turn left, through the doors, and you'll find Mr. Hanson's room about halfway down on the right-hand side. Here, I'll write his room number down for you."

Once up on the next floor, I went down the short corridor to Bruce's room. His bed was empty. "I'm sorry," said the nurse attending to the other patient in the semi. "Visiting hour are over, and Mr. Hanson is in the treatment room right now."

"May I leave this?" I asked.

"Yes, just leave it on his bedside table."

I tucked a card in the foliage. On it, I'd written, "Dear Bruce, With warm thoughts of you and to you. Meg."

I found a cafeteria in the main building of the hospital and bought a cup of coffee and a date square. The coffee was vile — a thin, bitter brew that Mrs. Hanson would have poured down the sink — and I couldn't finish it.

Once I was out of the hospital, I went back to Heather Street and stood there, looking up at what I thought must be Bruce's room. I caught a brief glimpse of a movement at the window. It was too far to see who was waving. But just in case — yes, please, Lord — it was Bruce, I waved back until my arm ached.

Chapter Twelve

THE CHRISTMAS HOLIDAYS were over. When I saw Jack at the bus stop, I wondered what had happened to him. He looked wild with his uncombed hair and purple shadows under his eyes.

As soon as we got in the classroom, he flipped up his desktop and started to throw things on the floor. He was swearing under his breath. Once, he kicked the desk.

"What's up, Jack?" I asked.

His voice was deep with bitterness. "My stepfather has made another one of his brilliant decisions. He's moving us into Vancouver. He and Mom are in there now, looking for a place to rent. That means starting a new school — which totals four in the last two years — and no one cares how it affects me. I hate the bastard."

"Oh, Jack! Sorry. We'll miss you. One day we'll read about your brilliant career in science and say, 'We knew he could do it.'"

"I'll write to you, Meg, and let you know my new address and phone number. When you come into Vancouver, we'll get together. Okay?"

I nodded. I would be sorry to see him go. It would be hard to keep up with chemistry on my own. But it was more than that. Amy gone. Bruce away. And now Jack.

Feb 7, 1945

Dear Bruce,

I hope you liked the poinsettia I left for you at the hospital. I wanted to visit you, but they said you were in the treatment room.

My brother's fiancée Olive, I told you about her, is a nurse, and she says the new drugs and dressings they're using are working miracles. I sure hope that's true and that your pain will be gone soon. I say a prayer every night for you. (I'm for anything that works.)

I'm trying to knit booties for Amy's baby. I've had to unravel them twice. I'm only going to try once more.

Your mother has a few mill workers boarding with her.

Most of them are single guys who are lonely and away from home. They rave about her cooking.

Love,
Meg

I wished I had enough nerve to visit Bruce, but I wasn't sure he'd want me to.

I missed him so much that I felt like I had swallowed a huge rock, one with jagged edges on it. Sometimes I couldn't stop tears from coming. I thought if I ever started crying, I would never be able to stop.

I was worried about him because his mother said, "Bruce is doing as well as can be expected," which could mean anything. I worried that he was in a lot of pain. I worried that he had a raging infection. I worried that the skin graft wasn't taking.

Most of all, I was almost sick thinking that he didn't really care for me, and it was all just wishful thinking on my part. Of course, why should he care? Then I felt so foolish. Pathetic. And I was torn up by the idea that I'd imagined that, somehow, I was special to him and that he did want us to be together in the future. What kind of skin graft was he having, anyway, that made this all so mysterious and serious? Had his burns made him somehow afraid to fall in love? Why? Did he think he was too disfigured? Maybe he couldn't have children? Or couldn't make love? Physically, I mean. I loved him anyway.

I decided that I would study even harder to fill up the big hole in my life. Before Jack left at the end of January, he had gone over all our correspondence chapters yet to be done and helped me make out study cards, and he chose lists of experiments I could do on my own. We checked it over with Mr. Freeman, and he was impressed.

"Well, Jack," he said. "It has been a pleasure to have you as my student. We all wish you the very best." Mr. Freeman never showed any emotion except cheerfulness, but I thought I saw a look of sadness in his eyes.

"You and Meg. You are two of the best students I've ever had. If all my students were as good, my life would be easy. Keep in touch, Jack. Let us know how you are doing. You will go on to do great things, I'm sure. If there is any way I can help, any way at all, please don't hesitate to ask."

A few days later after school, I stopped off at the Landing to pick up the daily mail. The *Lady Rose* was tying up at the wharf on her return trip to Vancouver, and, as usual, I went down to the wharf to see her off.

Jack stood by the gangway with a suitcase by his side, and I walked over to say goodbye. His body was stiff with anger, but I thought I saw more than that in his eyes, a softness, a vulnerability. He took my hand and said, "You did come down to say goodbye."

"I didn't know what day you were leaving," I said. "When I didn't see you at school, I thought it might be today."

He pressed something into my hand. It was a small, metal bar with a crest on it. "It's my school pin, from the year I went to Lord Byng. I want you to wear it."

I hesitated.

"This isn't goodbye for us, Meg."

He sounded so sincere that I felt like a fraud.

"Jack, uh, you know I like you, but I can't wear your pin. Wouldn't it mean we are going steady?"

"It only means that I'd like you to be my girlfriend. I know I won't be here. But, soon, we'll be together, in Vancouver once you're in nurses' training, and I'm at UBC. Take it. I'll write."

The ship's whistle sounded. Jack bent to kiss me. I turned my face away, and his kiss landed on my cheek. He started up the gangplank. The school pin in my hand pinched into my skin.

"Mom, I've decided I don't really like Jack. I mean, he's been a good friend to me, and kind, in many ways. But he's got a cold streak in him."

"He seems like a nice enough boy, Meg. And he's going to make something of himself. You could do a lot worse. What choice of young men do you have on the peninsula, anyway? Fishermen, loggers. So many of our young men away at war. What's left for you?" She paused. "Did you know that young Douglas Thompson is missing in action? I just heard. Poor Mrs. Thompson."

"Oh, no! How sad. I'll go over and see her."

Later that day, I brought up the subject of Jack with my mother again. "It's more than coldness, I think. He's so angry inside and so determined to have his own way, that it's kind of scary."

"We all have to put up with something from men. It's their nature . . . You'll find it pretty hard, Meg, to make it on your own. It's the way society's set up."

"But if I get my RN, then I *will* be able to make it on my own."

"As a spinster. If you ever decide to marry, you'll be out of a job."

"There's a shortage of nurses."

"Doesn't matter. The hospitals won't hire married nurses unless they have to. You have the choice to be independent with no husband and no children, or get married to someone with a future. Like Jack. You can always use your nurses' training to take care of your own children when they come. But Jack's family could be a problem. They sound unstable to me. And they're English, you say."

"Mom! We aren't prejudiced against the English here in Canada, the way you were back in Ireland."

"I'm just pointing out the facts, Meg. Marriage is tough enough as it is."

It made me think about marriage. I thought of all the married couples I knew in the Landing, and maybe Mom was right. There was always compromise, most often on the wife's part. Robert Pryce's wife looked the other way. Mr. Ballard forgave, but had he really? Mr. Miller stayed away. Mrs.

Hanson was widowed early. My own parents quarrelled; there were hints of other women. I couldn't think of one married couple that I could look at and say, "I hope my husband and I will be like that." I thought about marrying Bruce and decided our marriage would be different.

I wrote to Bruce every week, and every mail day I called in at the post office, hoping that there would be a letter from him.

Then one day in March, when purple violets grew in clumps between the rocks outside the post office, there was a letter from him. I had never seen Bruce's handwriting before, but his name and return address, Room 202, Heather Pavillion, Vancouver General Hospital, 2775 Heather Street, were on the left-hand corner of the front of the envelope.

I went back out into the bright spring sunlight, down to the beach, and found a quiet place to sit and savour the moment of holding his letter. His handwriting was like him, clear, decisive but not bold, like Jack's, whose handwriting on the few letters he'd written was pointed like daggers on their upward strokes.

I held Bruce's letter to my face, hoping to catch his smell. There was nothing but a paper smell. I opened the envelope, my breath catching.

March 1, 1945

Dear Meg,

I'm feeling better today and want to thank you for all your letters and for the poinsettia you left at Christmastime. It's still blooming on my bedside table, and I think of you every

*time I look at it. It is so bright and lovely in the sunshine,
just like you. It means a lot to me to have you care.*

*I won't bore you with the details of life here in the burn
unit. The important news is that the graft is finally
healing, and every day I see an improvement. The doctors
say that at the present rate of progress, I could be discharged
by summer.*

Keep well, dear one.
Bruce

I kissed his letter. The sun was surprisingly warm on my
face. Never had the sky been so pure a blue.

Chapter Thirteen

DURING THE EASTER HOLIDAYS, I was scheduled to work six days a week at the guest house, but Mrs. Thompson invited me to go into Vancouver with her. My mother said, "She's fretting about her son Doug, and now that her young boarder has gone, she's in a real slump. It would be good for her to have your company, Meg, and she likes you."

"I could visit Amy at the same time," I said. And Bruce, too, I thought.

I asked Mrs. Hanson about my taking a few days off from the guest house. "I'll work extra time for you before I go into Vancouver and again when I come back," I said.

"It's just that without Anna here, I'll be swamped. From

Good Friday on, is one of the busiest times of the year. I was counting on you."

"If I worked Thursday morning, went in on the noon boat and came back on the late boat on Friday? And I could come in a couple of hours early for you on Saturday morning."

"Yes," she said reluctantly, "I suppose that would work out ... But what's so important that you have to go into Vancouver?"

"Mrs. Thompson asked me to. And Mrs. Miller says that Amy is having a rough time. She's going to have a Caesarian early next week. I'd like to see her."

"Well ... All right, then. It's only Good Friday that you're missing ... When you're in Vancouver, do you think you'd have time to take something in to Bruce? I've made a parcel up for him, and it would cost a fortune to mail."

Of course, my main reason for wanting to go into Vancouver was to see Bruce. I caught the streetcar near Mrs. Thompson's apartment, and within an hour, was within walking distance of the burn unit at Vancouver General Hospital. The trees lining the streets smelled of sticky buds. Spring. I felt full of its promise. Though it was the end of March, and we should have been getting warm breezes from the south, the wind was cold. Snow on the mountains across Burrard Inlet glistened in the early morning sunlight.

I checked in with the receptionist on the main floor of Heather Pavillion and took the stairs two at a time up to the

Medical Floor. My heart pounded in my throat as I started down the polished corridor.

The door to Bruce's room was closed, a dressing cart parked outside. Around it were gathered a group of white-coated doctors. One of them began to read aloud from a chart. I spotted a wheelchair parked nearby and sat down in it to wait until the doctors had finished and gone. From where I sat, I could overhear much of what was said. A strong smell of Lysol permeated the air.

"This young naval officer suffered third-degree burns when torpedoed in the North Atlantic," droned the older doctor. "You will recall from your lectures that such a third-degree burn means charring and destruction of the tissues. You will remember that I said there is constitutional and local shock and toxemia with liver and kidney symptoms." He paused. "Gentlemen, let me emphasize that it is not the degree of the burns, but the extent of the skin surface that is the most important factor in recovery."

Just then, a cart holding several pitchers of water and fruit juices and pushed vigorously by a student nurse in a blue uniform, went out of control. It came rolling down the hallway and, gathering momentum, hit the wheelchair I sat in. Before I knew what was happening, the wheelchair spun around and crashed into the doctor's dressing cart.

I got up and fled, leaving astonished doctors staring after me. I kept walking rapidly until I found an open doorway. I ducked into it and found myself in a bathroom with urinals, toilets and sinks. I hid there until I had enough courage to peek around the doorway to see when I could safely leave.

Three student nurses were picking up broken glass. A senior nurse in a white uniform, starched bib and cuffs, was trying to placate the doctors. A janitor with a mop and bucket appeared.

I waited until the coast was clear, found an elevator at the opposite end of the hallway and punched the button repeatedly for the first floor.

"That was a short visit," said the receptionist, looking at me over her glasses.

"My friend was busy," I said. "I'll come back later."

I kept away for an hour, walking around and hoping the fresh air would calm me. This time when I went up to the second floor, I spotted Bruce through his open door. He was sitting up in bed, partially turned to the right, as if talking to his roommate.

I stayed where I was, letting the sound of his voice drift over me, like wood smoke.

"Meg! Meg!" Bruce called out.

I went in, and without thinking, put my arms around him. My tears were impossible to stop. I kept holding him.

"Let me see you," he said. "I need convincing you're really here."

In a moment, I pulled back, but I couldn't speak. I remembered the parcel his mother had sent and gave it to him. He put it aside, his eyes never leaving my face.

I began to tell him all of the news of the Landing. "The

Ballards are expecting another child. Yes! I guess they made up after all their troubles. Mr. Ballard seems happier about it than his wife. But then she's still not feeling well." I was talking too much. "And, oh, I've got my application for nurses' training with me — I'm going to drop it in at the School of Nursing this afternoon. I'll be down at St. Paul's anyway, visiting Amy. She's going to have a Caesarian section early next week."

"Come closer," he said.

I did.

"No, closer. I want to make sure you're really here." He took my hand and raised it to his lips. "Okay, now you can sit down."

I fumbled for the chair. I seemed to have lost all sensation in my legs. Had he any idea of how he made me feel?

I babbled on. "Oh, I forgot to mention. I'm staying with Mrs. Thompson at her apartment. She's worried about her son Doug."

"Come back here again, Meg."

A student nurse's head appeared around the doorway. "Mail for you this morning, Mr. Hanson," she said. She came in and handed Bruce a pale blue envelope. I could smell its perfume from where I sat.

Bruce let the envelope drop onto his bedside table. "I can look at that later. Thanks." The student left. Bruce said, "You're more important, Meg. Besides, I don't even recognize the handwriting."

"I do," I said, standing and craning my neck. "It's Amy's."

"Not likely." He frowned. "Why would she be writing me?"

He retrieved the envelope, opened it and took out a single sheet of matching blue paper. A snapshot fell out. The smell of perfume became even stronger in the air between us.

He read the letter, glanced at the snapshot and handed them both to me.

Dear Bruce,

I guess you are surprised to hear from me. You shouldn't be. I think of you often.

We're both patients in hospitals. You must be as lonely as I am.

I'd be glad to see you again.

Yours,
Amy

Okay. This is all right, I told myself. Almost. No. The photo was of Amy at her loveliest and most provocative. I had taken it early last summer with Amy's camera, when she was going through her movie star stage. This was her pose as Hedy Lamarr. She succeeded in looking like a beautiful, seductive woman.

Why would Amy do this? She must be out of her mind.

I let everything fall from my hand onto Bruce's bed.

"You should see your face, Meg. You're not very pleased."

"No, I'm not."

"Are you jealous? Don't be. That's Amy. No big surprise there."

He picked up the letter, envelope and photo and dropped them all into the wastebasket near his bed.

"Are you going to answer her letter?" I asked.

He laughed and motioned me to him. "You must be joking. You know me better than that, Meg. You're the one for me. If you'll have me."

I seethed all the way to St. Paul's. I decided to visit Amy on the maternity ward after I'd put in my application at the School of Nursing. I hoped to have calmed down by then. After all, Amy was a patient, and, I gritted my teeth, I shouldn't upset her.

A short flight of stairs led up to the doors of St. Paul's Nurses Home. Looking through the glass windows of the entrance door, I saw a statue of St. Paul. Student nurses in white uniforms passing in the hallway flitted back and forth in front of it.

Inside, and to the left, I found the main office. An elderly woman hovered over the students who were picking up their mail. She wore a long, grey sweater with drooping sleeves, and she picked nervously at the pins holding her grey hair in a bun. Her eyes were grey, too, making her whole appearance one of desolation. The students treated her with grave politeness until they got out into the hallway, and then they snorted laughter.

"Yes?" she said, acknowledging me in a querulous voice.

"I have my application for the September class," I said, handing her my large envelope.

She bared false teeth. "I'll tell Sister Mary Gertrude you are here," she said.

Alarmed, I said, "I thought I could just leave the application." I hadn't counted on being interviewed today. Would my feelings of anger with Amy show?

"Sister will want to see you. Wait in the room across the hall. I'll call you when Sister is ready ... Are you chewing gum?"

"No."

"Sister hates gum chewing."

The waiting room was small and square. I parked my gum in the earth of a large vase holding a potted fern. Religious pictures on all four walls inspected me gravely. A young man teetered on an uncomfortable-looking straight-backed chair and shuffled his feet back and forth. He was soon joined by a pretty girl, who had stepped out of the nearby elevator. For a moment, there was a brightness and joy in the room. After they left, the eyes of the painted saints on the wall stared down sternly.

The elderly woman stood before me, oxfords firmly planted on the floor. "Sister Mary Gertrude is ready to see you now," she said in an accusing voice. By this time, I was beginning to think that the whole idea of my entering nurses' school was not a good one.

Sister Mary Gertrude was a business-like woman in her late fifties, whose calm manner was reassuring. I thought that as long as I learned her rules and stayed within them, I'd be all right.

"I know young girls," she said after she had seated me across from the desk from her. "I know every trick they have in their book. Now, I have a few questions for you. First, let me look at your papers again." She shuffled through them quickly. "All of your qualifications are excellent, and your grades, too . . . What does your parish priest have to say about you, I wonder." She opened a desk drawer, pulled out a folder and quickly read a letter. "Ah, yes, Father Smith. I met him once. Deaf as a post." After a few minutes, she looked over at me. "He praises your mother and your brother, slams your father and has next-to-nothing to say about you. Why is that, do you think?"

"I'm sorry, I don't know."

"I don't know, Sister Mary Gertrude," she corrected.

"Yes. I'm sorry, I don't know, Sister Mary Gertrude."

"Could it be that you do not go to Sunday Mass regularly?"

"I work on weekends, yes," I said.

"We have daily Mass here at six a.m., and we expect all our Catholic girls to attend."

"Yes, Sister Mary Gertrude."

She went through my papers again. "We do have a three-month probation period, so we can ferret out those who are not suited to the nursing profession. Girls who do not put nursing first. Young women who party. Who get engaged."

She stood up abruptly. I scrambled to my feet. "That will be all," she said. "I will send you a formal letter of acceptance and a list of what you'll need to bring in with you. You may go now. I'll see you in September when you've graduated from high school."

"Thank you, Sister Mary Gertrude."

Amy was in tears when I went into her room on the maternity ward.

"I'm so glad to see you," she said. "Why does everything happen to me?"

"Are you talking about the Caesarian? That's to make sure that you and the baby are safe."

"No, I expected that. It's Glen. He's been tired for months. Now it turns out that he has TB. He's in the Willow Chest Centre at VGH, and he'll be there for at least a year. It means that he'll miss writing his finals at UBC."

"Oh. Can't the university work around that somehow? How long has he been in the Chest Centre?"

"Two weeks now. I haven't seen him all that time. Can't, of course. It's contagious. They think he got it from living with his aunt. You knew Robert's wife had TB?"

She had stopped crying and was studying my face. "You don't seem very sympathetic, Meg."

"I'm sorry Glen has TB. I just don't know what to say to you."

She sat back in bed, her eyes never leaving mine.

"I wrote Bruce Hanson, Meg." She waited, as if wanting me to speak. I didn't know how I was going to control my anger. "Maybe I shouldn't have done that," she said after a minute. "You're mad at me, aren't you? If you knew how lonely I felt the day I wrote the letter!"

"You're free to do whatever you want," I said. "But we're not friends anymore."

"Why? I told you, didn't I? It's not as if I tried to hide anything. I'll *need* you, Meg, when I go back to the Landing. I *have* to have friends."

"You knew how much Bruce meant to me, Amy."

"I forgot," she said, her face expressionless.

"There's always Louise, your best friend. And Robert Pryce," I said. "You can have them for friends."

"Yes, that's true." Amy's face brightened, then clouded. "You won't change your mind? You're being stubborn about this. It's not like you."

"Actually, it is like me. I have to be able to trust my friends."

"You mean that from now on you're going to be angry at me? Never talk to me again?"

"I'll talk to you. The way I'd talk to anyone else. Nothing more. It's just that I'm not your best friend anymore."

Chapter Fourteen

⚜

THE MONTH OF MAY brought sunshine and purple lilacs
that scented the air with their sweetness. Birds began to twit-
ter almost before the first light of morning showed at the
edge of my bedroom curtains. By the time the sun had risen,
the woods outside were full of bird song.

It was hard to believe it had just been a year since Amy and
I had found the first note in the woods and traced it back to
Rob Pryce. Perhaps it was because I felt alive and glowing
with love for Bruce that this spring seemed lovelier than ever.
Even the leaves on the trees took on the shape of Bruce.

Amy's baby girl had been born with a congenital heart
defect and had been transferred to Children's Hospital right

after her birth. Glen was still in Willow Chest. Amy had come back to the Landing to stay with her mother.

"She's what they call a 'blue baby,'" Amy said. "The doctors hope to repair her heart when she's a little older. They say that Johns Hopkins is having success with a new operation. The babies become pink again."

"It must be hard for you not to have her with you," I said.

Amy thought about it. "No, not really. She looked so blue and all wrinkled up when I first saw her that I didn't really believe she was mine . . . She's not the kind of baby I'd pictured having."

"What's her name?" I asked.

"Helen. I named her after Glen's mother. He wanted me to."

As soon as Amy felt strong enough, she and Rob Pryce drove back to Ontario to visit Glen's father. "Once the old man meets me, he'll change his mind," Amy said. "He's got piles of money. There's no reason why he couldn't be helping Glen and me. Rob and I will stay with him for a couple of weeks. That should be enough time for me to win him over."

"Or not," I said.

She looked at me, surprise sharpening her eyes. "You'll see," she said, confidently. "I have a way of changing men's minds. In the meantime, Rob and I can have a holiday. All this visiting TB patients back and forth is getting to us."

"How is Rob's wife?"

"She's okay," she said. "She'll be at Tranquille for at least a year."

Provincial exams were coming up in June, and I had been studying for months. I had written the provincials in math and English in grade eleven, but now French, science and history loomed. With Bruce still in the hospital, studying helped take my mind off missing him.

We wrote each other often, and at last came the letter with the news I'd been waiting for.

May 8, 1945

Dearest Meg,

Good news at last. The war in Europe is over finally, VE Day. Victory over Japan will follow soon, I'm sure.

Vancouver is celebrating. Fireworks have been going off all day long. The air is blue with their smoke, and it smells of sulphur. One of the nurses took the few of us who are well enough down to Broadway to watch the parade. There were streamers, confetti and girls riding on the tops of cars. Talk about noise! Bagpipes, trumpets, cornets, drums — even old pots were being banged. Everybody was kissing everybody else. When people weren't kissing, they were cheering.

More good news: the doctors say I will be discharged soon from the hospital. They are pleased with my recovery, and so am I. Most important, everything is working again.

Other than some shiny-looking patches on my skin, the
results are even better than I had hoped for.

Can't wait to see you again.

All my love,
Bruce

My brother, Sam, came home on a brief leave. "As soon as the paperwork goes through with my honourable discharge, I'll be registering at UBC," he told us, as we sat around the supper table. "The Department of Veterans Affairs has a plan where all veterans can go on to complete their education. I'm going after a degree in engineering. We'll receive a living allowance too, so Olive and I can get married and . . . It looks like I have a future, after all."

He said that he'd met Dad recently in Halifax and that Dad was in no hurry to be discharged. "He says he wants to stay in the Air Force," Sam said.

"The pay's good," said Mom. "And the wife's allotment cheque is regular every month."

"Dad likes the Air Force," said Sam. "It suits him. He gets to travel, and all that."

"And 'all that' is right," said my mother and let the subject drop.

Mrs. Thompson came to visit us shortly after Sam's leave was over. She was holding a letter up to her heart. "It's from the government," she said. Her cheeks were flushed pink, her eyes shining. "They've located my son Douglas. He's been released from a prisoner-of-war camp in Germany. My prayers are answered, and I've been on my knees thanking God ever since I got the letter."

"His girlfriend will be happy," I said.

"What girlfriend?"

"Didn't he have one from Maple Creek? I thought she came to the coast with Doug to visit you once."

"Oh, did she? I guess that one didn't last."

Jack Whalan had written a couple of times since he'd moved into Vancouver, and I had answered, trying to keep my letters friendly, but nothing more. Then I got a letter that made me realize I had to set things straight.

June 15, 1945

Dear Meg,

I'm still writing exams, but when they're over, I'm coming up your way and want to see you.

I've signed on as chokerman for the summer with a logging camp up Egmont and Earl's Cove way. I should make enough cash to pay for tuition at UBC. I'll have to get another job once I'm at university to pay for board and room. I'll try the library.

*I'd like to see you either before I start the job, or after I
finish. I think the logging outfit is running a bus service
out of Sechelt to Gibson's, so I'll walk down to your place
from there.*

*Are you wearing my pin? Please answer this question.
If you're not, I'd like it back.*

Jack

I mailed Jack's pin back to him on the next boat. I enclosed
a note saying that I'd started going with someone. I wished
him well at UBC.

On the last day of school, as I was heading to catch the bus
home, I heard my name being called. I turned to see Bruce
parked under the maple trees nearby. He got out of his truck
and came over to take the pile of books from my arms. I had
forgotten how handsome he was. I fell in love with him all
over again.

"I thought you might like a ride home," he said.

"I didn't know you were back." I was glad that I'd sham-
pooed my hair the night before and was wearing a sweater
he'd once said he liked.

Instead of turning the truck left to go home to the Landing, Bruce took the road down to Gower Point and parked
above one of the secluded beaches. We took the trail down to
the water. Through the trees, we could see glimpses of Vancouver Island, blue in the distance.

Halfway down the trail, Bruce stopped. "Wait, Meg. I have to talk to you." His eyes and face looked concerned, almost anxious. "It's important. I have to be fair to you ... I don't think you know what you're getting into."

"With you, you mean?"

"Yes. You know I care about you. I've had all the plastic surgery available, and I can have children. It's time to think about a future together. I will be able to take care of you."

I started to say something.

"No, I want you to become a nurse so that you'll always have a profession. The big question is ... could you love me?" He paused for the briefest of seconds. "Physically? You may not want to once you see my burns."

"Well, are you going to show me now?" I said.

His head jerked back.

"There's no one around," I said. "Let's see what you're talking about."

His eyes were startled, and I was afraid I'd gone too far. Then he unbuttoned his shirt and let it drop to the trail.

A width of chest, shiny pink patches of healed skin, well-developed muscles — I could imagine the strength of his arms holding me.

"Okay, now turn around," I said.

A long back. No burns. It's length arching over me.

"You can put your shirt back on again," I said.

He'd buttoned it. I said, "Okay, now the pants. Drop them. Front and back views, please."

By this time, he was laughing.

"I have to see what you have to offer," I said.

He unbuckled his belt and let the pants drop, stepped out of them.

A slim waist, flat abdomen showing a recently healed shiny spot, long muscled legs. I seemed to have stopped breathing. He turned. Tight buttocks.

"Okay," I managed. "You can dress now."

When he had tucked his shirt in and checked his fly, I put my arms around him. He pulled me in closer. "What do you think, Meg?"

"There'll be no problem," I said. "Unless I've scared you off."

He kissed me then. I had thought about it so often, but I had never imagined it would feel so completely right. The gulls called out from the ocean below. *O-kaay. O-kaay.* Meg loves Bruce. Bruce loves Meg.

July and August were our months to get to know each other. I saw him often during the day as I went about my work at the guest house. In the afternoon, I had a couple of free hours, and we swam, hiked or went out in the boat. Friday-night dances, we went together as a couple. Frank Sinatra had recorded "Day by Day," and it became our song.

"I'm glad we have this time," Bruce said. "Once we both start hitting the books in the fall, we'll see each other, but it won't be as often. This summer belongs to us."

Mrs. Hanson approved, Anna Hanson approved, even my

mother approved. "You'll be busy enough, once you start working in the hospital on the wards. Enjoy this time while you can."

The evening before Bruce and I left the Landing for Vancouver, we went out in his boat. Once we were well off shore, Bruce cut the engine, and we drifted on the crimson and gold ocean that reflected the sunset. Bruce said, "I'd like to give you an engagement ring. You could pick it out at Birks. That's if you're still sure about us."

"I'm sure. But let's leave the ring until I'm almost finished training. Sister Mary Gertrude made it clear that she expects her student nurses to put nursing first, no distractions . . . I don't think I can wait three years to marry you, but I guess I'll have to."

Bruce and I married as soon as I had written my RN exams. I signed up with the private duty registry of the hospital. They hired married nurses, and I could choose my shifts.

We were each other's best friend then, and we are each other's best friend today.

Epilogue

AMY'S DAUGHTER HELEN died before she was a year old.

Glen was pronounced cured of TB and discharged after a year at Willow Chest Centre.

Six months later, Robert Pryce's wife died in the TB Sanitarium at Kamloops from a lung haemorrhage. Robert sold their house and moved away. No one was sure where. The village settled down to its former rhythm.

Glen and Amy went to the States to live. Glen's father never gave his consent to their marriage, and they had to wait until Glen was twenty-one before they married. Whether the father ever helped them financially was never mentioned, but the two of them seemed to manage all right. After the marriage, they had two healthy sons. Glen became a well-known TV personality. They divorced, and he married three more times with children by each wife. Amy never remarried.

Amy and I were friendly when we met, which was sporadic, but never in the same way we'd been in high school.

Mrs. Miller, invalid though she'd been when I first met her, lived into her nineties. She kept her sweetness and ability to make friends until the end.

Mr. and Mrs. Ballard had a little boy they adored.

My father stayed away for longer and longer periods until finally he didn't come home at all. Mom became very active in the church.

Mrs. Thompson sold their place and got a larger apartment in Vancouver. Doug never married and lived with her.

Jack Whalan went on for his PhD and made a major contribution to early work on DNA. He sent me postcards off and on throughout the years, always to do with his scientific interests and achievements.

Anna and her husband moved into the guest house to help Mrs. Hanson run it.

Bruce made a career in the Navy and held a position of high command. I worked as a nurse in cities on both sides of the country. We have two children.

ABOUT THE AUTHOR

PHOTO: CHUNG CHOW

When Mary's three children were in high school, she took a night school course in creative writing offered by the Vancouver School Board and sold an article written in that class. Encouraged, she became a part-time student at the University of British Columbia, studied writing under George McWhirter and wrote an adult novel in a tutorial with Carol Shields. This novel was later rewritten as *Snow Apples*, for young adults, and shortlisted for the Governor General's Award. She went on to have ten more books published, many of them award-winning. Mary's poetry, articles and short stories have been published and broadcast internationally. She has a broad working background in both medical and surgical nursing and was the project worker for an oral history of nursing in B.C. She makes her home in Vancouver, B.C.

MARQUIS

Québec, Canada

RECYCLED
Paper made from
recycled material
FSC® C103567